"I haven't been able to stop thinking about that night."

"Carrick, please stop talking about it."

He moved closer to her and she could feel his heat. "Why? Because you regret it or because talking about it makes you hot?"

"It's best if we just forget about that night." She gripped her hands behind her back and stepped away to put a solid amount of space between her and the star of some very X-rated dreams.

"I don't think that is going to happen anytime soon. I want you, Sadie. I know that we shouldn't, that we said it was a onetime thing, but then you walk into the room and all I can think about is being inside you as soon as possible...

"And judging by all that blue fire in your eyes, by the way they keep going to my mouth, racing over my body, I think you want that, too."

* * *

One Little Indiscretion by Joss Wood is part of the Murphy International series.

Dear Reader,

In my last book of the Love in Boston series, *Second Chance Temptation*, I introduced you to Tanna Murphy, the youngest sibling of the famous Murphy clan, owners of the world-renowned international auction house Murphy International.

One Little Indiscretion is the story of Carrick Murphy, the eldest of the Murphy siblings. Carrick's previous marriage ended in ugly accusations and resulted in too much press attention, so he's wary of commitment and is happy to keep his relationships brief and surface-based. And he never mixes business with pleasure...

So Carrick's attraction to divorcée Dr. Sadie Slade, the art detective he's hired to prove the provenance of a possible lost work of art, is an unwelcome distraction. After Sadie returns from the hospital after a choking incident, they both fall into temptation and sleep together, agreeing that a one-night stand is all they can have.

But that one night leads to long-term consequences, and Carrick and Sadie have to work through their issues around marriage, perception and independence before they can risk taking another chance on love.

I hope you enjoy the start to this brand-new series.

Happy reading!

Joss

Xxx

Connect with me on:

Facebook: JossWoodAuthor

Twitter: JossWoodbooks

BookBub: joss-wood

JOSS WOOD

———

ONE LITTLE INDISCRETION

HARLEQUIN®
DESIRE™

Recycling programs
for this product may
not exist in your area.

ISBN-13: 978-1-335-20892-7

One Little Indiscretion

Copyright © 2020 by Joss Wood

This edition published by arrangement with Harlequin Books S.A.

For questions and comments about the quality of this book, please contact us at CustomerService@Harlequin.com.

Harlequin Enterprises ULC
22 Adelaide St. West, 40th Floor
Toronto, Ontario M5H 4E3, Canada
www.Harlequin.com

Printed in U.S.A.

Joss Wood loves books and traveling—especially to the wild places of southern Africa and, well, anywhere. She's a wife, a mom to two teenagers and slave to two cats. After a career in local economic development, she now writes full-time. Joss is a member of Romance Writers of America and Romance Writers of South Africa.

Books by Joss Wood

Harlequin Desire

Murphy International

One Little Indiscretion

Love in Boston

Friendship on Fire
Hot Christmas Kisses
The Rival's Heir
Second Chance Temptation

Dynasties: Secrets of the A-List

Redeemed by Passion

Texas Cattleman's Club: Inheritance

Rich, Rugged Rancher

Visit her Author Profile page at Harlequin.com, or josswoodbooks.com, for more titles.

You can also find Joss Wood on Facebook, along with other Harlequin Desire authors, at Facebook.com/harlequindesireauthors!

Prologue

1. Mountain Climbing. (Thanks, altitude sickness.)
2. Marriage. (Nope. Once was more than enough.)
3. Riding a mechanical bull, like she had during Spring Break. (Four tequilas and being bucked like a rag doll resulted in the nickname "Pukey" for months.)
4. Oh, and lusting after Carrick Murphy. (That was the biggest no-no of all.)

Sadie Slade added having an emergency tracheotomy to her mental Things-I-Never-Intend-To-Do-Again list and touched the small gauze dressing on her neck. She'd never been more scared in her life.

Back in her apartment after an overnight stay in

the hospital, Sadie took a couple of deep breaths—
beautiful air!—and took stock. The doctors had as-
sured her that the temporary lack of oxygen when
she'd choked at the Murphy cocktail party the evening before hadn't compromised her mental faculties.
But she recited the facts anyway.

She was twenty-nine years old, had a PhD in art
history, owned her own business providing art valu-
ation and provenance tracking. Her best friend was
an Arabian prince she'd met in college. Another good
friend, Beth, was also her virtual assistant and business manager. Sadie was in Boston to track down the
provenance of what might be a lost Winslow Homer
painting for Murphy International.

And ever since she'd taken the job, she'd been trying to deal with her annoying desire for the sexy CEO
of Murphy International, Carrick Murphy—he of the
ripped body and gorgeous face but terrible reputation.

Why couldn't she be attracted to a guy who was
both successful and honorable, someone she could
respect? For once in her life she wanted to fall in lust
with someone who wasn't a player, cheater or weasel.

Apart from the inconvenience of imagining Murphy naked, she was fine.

Sadie flopped back in her chair and covered her
eyes with her forearm. Last night, before the ambu-
lance arrived, she'd kept her gaze firmly focused on
Carrick's face. His eyes were an unusual shade of
grape-green, shot with gold and silver and surrounded
by a ring of forest green.

Those amazing eyes rested in a face that was deliciously masculine—strong brows and jaw, a once straight nose that had, obviously, at one point been broken and was ever so slightly crooked, a stern but sexy mouth and a body able to make angels weep.

He was tall and ripped. And smart.

All excellent qualities…

Except for the fact that he was a carbon copy of her ex-husband. Or so she'd been informed by Beth, who was Carrick's ex-sister-in-law.

Sadie tried to avoid the type, after having separated from and then divorced her own philandering, work-obsessed penis of a partner. So when Murphy International approached her to investigate the authenticity of what could be a lost Winslow Homer painting, she'd seriously considered turning down their request.

Purely because she was violently allergic to rich, entitled, sexy men who believed they could do what they wanted, when they wanted, with no thought to who they hurt.

But emotions didn't pay the bills, and her business brain insisted that it was an offer she couldn't turn down. Murphy International was one of the top three auction houses in the world, with mega-rich and established clients. The company commanded power and respect in the art world, and consulting for them would be a solid gold star on her résumé.

So she'd temporarily relocated from Paris to her hometown of Boston and, as she'd expected, going to work at Murphy International, seeing Carrick Murphy every day, was pure torture.

Because, when she was in Carrick's company she forgot about his past—forgot that he was the type of man she avoided, that he'd been a miserable husband to a woman she called a friend. Instead, she enjoyed his sharp mind, his acerbic wit and his gorgeous looks.

When she was alone, she either fantasized about him being naked or castigated him for being a philandering, made-his-ex-miserable jerk.

Veering from lust to disdain and back again was freakin' exhausting. But as much as she wished she could blame all her exhaustion on her troublesome attraction to Murphy, it was nearly dying that had pushed this volcanic tide of mixed emotions to the surface.

Gratitude, fear, loneliness, vulnerability...

Sadie slid down farther on her sofa and closed her eyes. One way to avoid facing herself, and those pesky emotions she usually ignored, was to slip into sleep...

After Carrick had been banging on her door for a couple of minutes—he'd seriously considered applying his size thirteen foot to the lock—Sadie opened the door to her apartment, looking a little dazed and a lot sexy.

She'd been sleeping. There was a crease from a cushion on her cheek and her eyes were foggy. He should feel bad for waking her up, she'd had twenty-four hours from hell, but he was so damn grateful to see her standing, to hear her breathing, to look into her Persian-blue eyes.

Seeing the terror in all that blue the night before had scared the crap out of him.

Carrick stepped back to look at her, his hand gripping the jamb. He had no connection to her except through work, but for the first time in eighteen hours, his heart stopped careening around his chest cavity and settled down.

He didn't have the slightest clue why she affected him this way, this woman he barely knew. It had to be because she was sort of a Murphy employee and he felt tangentially responsible for her. That was the only reason he could come up with because they didn't have an emotional connection.

He didn't do connections, emotional or otherwise.

Not for a long time and not ever again.

"Hi," Sadie murmured. "Carrick? Um, why are you here?"

"Just checking up on you." He'd been aiming for casual but missed it by a mile.

"You look…" Carrick stumbled again, searching for the correct word. She was dressed in a red, off-the-shoulder, slouchy sweater over black leggings, and fluffy black socks. Her face was makeup free and her hair was tied up in a messy tail. A tiny dressing covered the cut on her throat.

He'd never seen anyone more beautiful. And, God, alive…

Sadie stepped back to allow him into the apartment. "Sorry, I'm a hot mess. I wasn't expecting company. Come in."

Why did women think being a hot mess was a bad thing?

Sadie shut the door behind him and looked down to the huge bouquet of flowers he carried. He wasn't sure what she liked so he'd told the florist to give her everything. The result was a riot of color and fragrance.

"Are those for me?"

Well, yes. Of course.

Carrick nodded and when he handed it over, Sadie disappeared behind the blooms and the greenery. No, he needed to see her face, to keep looking at her...

Why?

This wasn't like him and he didn't understand it. Long and happily divorced, he marched to the beat of his own drum, had no time for complicated emotions and didn't do clarifications, explanations or elaborations, to himself or to others.

He loved and protected his siblings and was loyal to the few close friends he had...

But Sadie Slade was neither family nor friend. So why was he reacting like this?

Sadie looked at him across the heads of the multicolored blooms. "Are you planning on talking to me?"

Talking was overrated; he could get his point across in other ways. Pulling the expensive bouquet from her arms, he dropped it to the floor. He hesitated for a moment, waiting for her to protest. When none came, he covered her mouth with his, drinking in her heat, her spice…her goddamn alive-ness.

Carrick moved her back so that she rested against the wall and then rested his palm against the cool plaster above her head. He wouldn't touch her with anything but his mouth. Because if he did, he wouldn't stop until he had her naked, panting and screaming his name.

Sadie had no problem using her hands, and he felt her tugging his shirt from his pants, and then her hands were on the bare skin above his belt, skimming across his spine. Every muscle in his body contracted and he wondered where all the oxygen in the room had gone.

But it didn't matter because Sadie was kissing him. And kissing him with a lot of enthusiasm.

Sadie's tongue pushed into his mouth and she wrapped her arms around his waist, silently telling him that she wanted him—this—as much as he did. Unable to keep his hands to himself, not for one more second, he floated his palm across the bare skin revealed by her oversize sweater and marveled at the softness. Would she be this soft everywhere?

"Touch me, Carrick," Sadie murmured. Her breathy words, punctuated by kisses, was all the encouragement he needed. He pulled her sweater up so he could access her fragrant skin. No bra, thank God. Dropping his head to kiss her throat, he told her exactly what he wanted to do to, and with, her.

Her excited, low pitched murmurs encouraged him to do all that. And more.

When she pulled his hand up to cover her breast, he groaned at the feel of her taut nipple pushing into his hard palm. Needing to taste her, Carrick pulled her sweater up and over her head, looking down at sheer perfection when she was exposed to his hot gaze.

Firm, high breasts, pretty pink nipples...

"I can't wait to taste you." Carrick bent his head and laved her with his tongue before sucking her into his mouth. Perfection. Carrick moved on to her other breast and after paying it the same attention, stood up and tunneled his fingers into her hair. "I want to take you to bed."

Sadie reached up to hold his wrist with her hand. "I know."

Carrick bent down to lean his forehead against hers. "That's not a yes, Sadie."

Sadie took his hand and led him down the hallway to her bedroom. Inside that china-blue and white space, she pushed her pants down her hips, taking her underwear with them. Stepping out of her socks, she stood before him, naked.

"Make love to me, Carrick. You make me feel so damn..."

Hot? Horny? Turned on?

"Alive," Sadie whispered. "I so very badly need, right now, to feel alive."

He could give that to her. And so he did.

One

Carrick Murphy heard the snick of the lock on the bathroom door and turned his head to bury his face in Sadie's sweet-smelling pillow.

Hell.

When he left his historic Beacon Hill house last night, his intention had been to check up on Murphy's new art investigator. Because, as he told himself repeatedly on the drive to her apartment, he only needed her in a professional capacity. He needed her skills to authenticate a painting so that the possible lost Homer could be included in their much-anticipated, once-in-a-generation auction happening in the spring. He'd brought her flowers—they were still on the floor in the hallway, probably dying—as a gesture from a client to a consultant, desperately trying to convince himself that his visit had nothing to do with Sadie being sexier than sin.

Great snow job, Murphy. Not your usual style, dude.

Releasing a frustrated huff, Carrick looked around for his clothes. The least he could do to make this morning less awkward was to be dressed when Sadie eventually decided to leave the bathroom.

He found his underwear by the door and pulled on his boxer briefs. They'd started shedding clothes in the hallway, a minute after their lips collided.

Not seeing any more of his clothes in the immediate vicinity, Carrick followed the garment trail through her apartment and plucked one of her socks off the frame of a black-and-white print and picked up her yoga pants and thong off the hallway floor. He found his shirt by the gray couch and his pants behind it.

Carrick pulled on his pants and then his button-down shirt, leaving the shirt open as he pulled on his socks, then his shoes. He eyed the door, wishing he could just slip out. But Sadie wasn't some woman he'd never see again and he wouldn't do that to her.

Since he was no longer a kid, he didn't leave without at the very least a "thank you," and even if it wasn't world-rocking sex, an "it was fun."

But it had been world-rocking sex and he would see Sadie later since he was paying her an exorbitant figure for her expertise to authenticate a painting. He needed her...

But *only* on a professional basis.

He'd trained himself not to need anyone anymore.

Since divorcing Tamlyn, he always thought long and hard about whom he slept with and the potential fallout—would the woman take her story to the press? Would she spread a rumor or four about the way he treated her? But his need for Sadie had drowned out all his fears and considerations.

He'd wanted her. She'd wanted him back. His brain had shut down after that...

But man, he hoped she didn't think this was the start of something special, that they were going anywhere. The worst outcome would be her catching *feelings*, wanting or expecting more from him than he could give.

Because he didn't have it in him.

He'd lost too many women he loved and cared about—his real mom, stepmom and sister-in-law to death, another sister-in-law to divorce—and his own divorce had drained him of any hopes and dreams and trust he had in a happy-ever-after, in having a family, a partnership, a wife he'd grow old with.

The closer someone became, the more they could hurt him. His ex was proof of that.

Carrick rubbed his hands over his face.

Yep, Tamlyn had soured him so he didn't bother dating, preferring an occasional, discreet, low-key one-nighter here and there. Sure, the sex was never as good as it could be in a committed relationship with a solid emotional connection...

Yet, it had been. With Sadie.

With Sadie, he'd forgotten that he hardly knew

her, that this was their first time. Making love to her was as natural as breathing; his body—dammit!—recognized hers. There had been no awkward fumbling, no indecision, no do-you-like-this?

She'd murmured her approval whenever she could speak, either by her breathy moans, low do-that-again groans or one-word sentences. The words *yes!* and *more!* had fallen from her lips with regularity.

The hell of it was, Sadie was the best he'd ever had, better even than those first heady days with Tamlyn.

Sadie, and their night together, exceeded all his expectations and set the bar space-high for his next one-night stand.

If he ever had another one of those again...

Carrick stood up and headed for the small galley kitchen on the other side of this open-plan, generic, boring-as-hell apartment. The least he could do was get the coffee started.

Carrick changed the filter on the machine, dumped in some coffee and topped up the water. After flipping the switch, he walked back into the living room and picked up her shirt from the pile he'd made on her coffee table. He lifted the soft fabric to his nose, inhaling her scent. She smelled like sunshine and warm wind and, underneath it all, a scent he couldn't identify. What he knew for sure was that it was a scent designed to make his head swim.

"Are you actually sniffing my shirt?"

Crap. Busted. The only option was to go on the offensive.

"What is this scent?" he demanded—casually, he

hoped—dropping the shirt to the pile. "It's driving me crazy."

"Jasmine and orange blossom," Sadie replied. She'd showered; her wet hair was raked back from her face. In faded jeans and a loose cranberry-colored sweater, she looked younger than her years.

"Remind me to buy you ten years' supply."

Sadie smiled, reluctantly charmed. "I wish you could. But the perfumer refuses to make big batches and only opens his shop in Montparnasse when he's in the mood. And he's frequently not in the mood."

Her eyes flickered over his bare chest, bracketed by his open shirt. He started to button up, but suddenly dropped his hands, and Sadie suspected he was enjoying her appreciation. He was a smart, experienced guy, and he'd obviously noticed the desire in her eyes, the heated flush on her cheeks.

There would be no round two—why complicate this further?—and he probably assumed that a little mutual appreciation couldn't hurt anyone.

He was wrong; this type of thing could lead to lots of pain down the line.

Play it cool, Sadie, and for goodness' sake, resist the urge to touch that wide chest. Find something else to do with your hands!

Breakfast. She could make breakfast…

Smart thinking, Slade.

"I understand you have an apartment in Paris," Carrick said, following her to the kitchen, watching as she pulled croissants, butter and jam from the fridge.

"I have a rabbit's hutch in Montparnasse, a tiny one-room apartment just big enough for me and my clothes and my reference books." Sadie gave him an up-and-down look. "You would look like Gulliver in Lilliput in it."

"Gulliver? Lilliput?" Then his face cleared and the penny dropped. "Right, Jonathan Swift's *Gulliver's Travels.*"

"Sorry, I'm a book nerd. And an art nerd. And a useless facts nerd."

"I like nerds. They are some of my favorite people," Carrick said, looking at her like she was the hottest nerd he'd ever seen. But that had to be her imagination...

"My brother Finn is the king of obscure references and trivia. I'm used to hearing odd bits of useless information," Carrick told her.

Noticing that the coffee was nearly ready, Carrick looked around the kitchen and asked where she kept her cups. After opening the cupboard she directed him to, he pulled out two mugs and filled them while Sadie placed warmed croissants on plates and pulled flatware out of a drawer.

She gestured to a stool on the other side of the island and Carrick sat down, immediately reaching for a warm buttery pastry.

Look at her, being all adult about this. And yeah, it wasn't as awkward as she'd expected it to be.

But as sophisticated as she was acting—presumably Carrick, having the morning-after-the-night-before routine down to a fine art, was being his normal self—

she needed to say something, anything, to make it clear that they were on the same page, that this was a one-time deal.

But Sadie was so out of her comfort zone. She didn't routinely jump into bed with strange men. And she never slept with people she worked with. And she never, ever slept with men—like her ex and, supposedly, Carrick Murphy—who treated women, and sex, like playthings…

That thought was obliterated by Carrick's next sentence. "So that shouldn't have happened."

That was her line!

Carrick popped a piece of strawberry jam-smeared croissant into his mouth, chewed and swallowed. He took another big bite, obviously enjoying the flaky pastry and tart jam.

"I came around to check up on you, but obviously we got a bit carried away," Carrick said in that genial tone that set her teeth on edge. "I hope it won't affect our working relationship."

What exactly did he mean by that? Did he think that, in her mind, sex equaled a relationship? She was a modern woman, fully capable of separating sex and emotion, carnality and commitment. She was in no danger of falling for him after one night of fantastic, mind-blowing sex. She'd heard that he'd left a trail of broken hearts and disappointed damsels throughout Boston, but she wasn't that weak.

Not anymore.

"I'm sure we'll be just fine," Sadie stated, her tone

firm. "As long as you realize that nothing but the evidence will affect my findings on the Homer."

Carrick placed the corner of his croissant on his plate, reached for his coffee cup and she saw the flash of temper in his eyes. "Why the hell would you think that I'd expect you to fudge results on the painting, to tell me what you think I'd want to hear? The art speaks for itself. It always has and it always will."

That hadn't been true for her ex. Dennis's moral line was exceptionally fluid and he hadn't hesitated to use any means to influence the outcome of a deal, or a relationship, to benefit himself. Sure, it was only one brief sentence, but in this regard, she believed Carrick Murphy wasn't like her ex.

It shouldn't be a relief but...yes, it was.

From a business standpoint—the only standpoint that mattered—his integrity made her job easier.

But getting back to why he was in her kitchen in the early hours of a Monday morning...

"Well, going forward, I suggest we forget that last night happened. It was fun—" so much fun! "—but I have a job to do and a repeat performance isn't in the cards."

"It would just be too complicated," Sadie blithely added, hoping she looked as casual as she sounded.

Carrick took another sip of coffee and tightened his fingers around the handle of the mug. "Okay, if that's how you feel."

No, it wasn't! Yes, it was... Arrgh! She didn't know what to feel! All she knew was that the last time she'd hopped into bed with a charming man, she'd had her life torn apart. She could never, ever let that happen again.

Sadie pulled apart her croissant and nibbled the inside of her cheek. God, she wished he'd just leave, give her some space, some time to make sense of nearly losing her life and having great sex and a hot guy in her kitchen at still-dark o'clock.

Reaching across the island, Carrick gripped her wrist, his fingers tan against her paler skin.

"Sadie, look at me."

Sadie tossed her damp hair and sucked in a deep breath before obeying his soft order. Her eyes slammed into his and she had to remind herself to breathe.

Carrick's smile was gentle, as sweet as a tough, masculine man could make it. "Thank you for an amazing night. I hope you enjoyed it as much as I did."

She had. Best night spent naked...*ever*.

"I should be off. Murphy International won't, unfortunately, run itself."

Sadie knew she should feel relieved, or even happy, at hearing that he was on his way, but she only felt disappointment. Which was stupid because not a couple of minutes ago she'd wanted to be alone.

Carrick released her wrist and started to do up the buttons on his shirt. Standing, he tucked his shirttails into his pants and popped the last piece of croissant into his mouth. "Damn, these are amazing."

Walking around the island, he looked down into her face and Sadie held her breath as he lowered his head, aiming his lips at her mouth. Catching himself, he jerked back.

"I'm really glad you are fine after your choking incident."

Thank God for his sister Tanna's quick thinking or she wouldn't be here, home from the hospital and exhausted after a night of being well loved.

Very well loved indeed.

Carrick used his knuckle to tip up her chin and look at the sterile gauze low down on her neck. "Is it painful?"

Sadie shook her head. "The cut is tiny and it'll heal fast." Sadie pulled a face. "Though I am considering becoming a vegetarian."

Carrick smiled at her dejected tone. "It could've happened as easily with a piece of carrot as it did a piece of steak."

"Point taken, but it might still be a while before I feel brave enough to swallow down another piece of rare Kobe beef. Or any meat at all."

"Completely understandable." Carrick looked at his watch and winced at the time. "I need to get going. I have a nine o'clock meeting and I still have to get home and shower."

"You could take a shower here," Sadie quietly offered. "If that saves you some time."

She waited while he thought about it, knowing that if he made the slightest suggestion that she join him, she'd find it incredibly hard to hold herself to her have-touched-him-for-the-last-time decision. And if he stayed longer, she might just pull him into the shower herself and do several things to him she hadn't thought of last night.

Hot, carnal, X-rated things...

"Thanks, but I'm good. I'm going to head straight for the office and hit the showers in the company gym. I keep a change of clothing and toiletries in the executive bathroom I share with my brothers, so fresh clothes won't be a problem."

Sadie followed him as he walked toward the hallway, taking a moment to admire the tight butt that now knew the shape and feel of her fingertips.

"I take it you're not coming in today. You probably need time to recover."

"I spent the night making love to you, Carrick, so I can hardly pull the 'I'm sick' card," Sadie replied with a touch of tart. "But I am going to work from home today, trawling the net for anything I can find on Homer's time in Virginia. And then I'm heading to an art gallery on Charles Street since Isabel Mounton-Matthews did a lot of business with the previous owner. I'm hoping to find something about the painting in the sale catalogs or records."

Carrick asked her the name of the gallery and she told him, comfortable now that they were talking art.

"I'm aware of the gallery. The grapevine has it that both the past and the present owners haven't always been on the up and up. Apparently, they have the reputation for fudging provenances or filling in the missing information with a little creative wording."

"Thanks. I'll keep it in mind."

"I wouldn't call them shady, but they aren't honest,

either. I don't think you have a hope in hell of seeing their records, if they keep decent records at all."

It was a fair point, but she needed to check. Just in case. Besides, she thought they could both do with some distance, time apart to get their heads on straight before they laid eyes on each other again.

With a little space they—she—would stop thinking about a repeat bedroom performance.

"So I'll see you again when I have a solid update. That might be days or even weeks from now," Sadie told him.

Carrick picked up her now-bedraggled and sad-looking bunch of flowers and laid them on the hall table. "I won't feel offended if you toss these."

It was obvious Carrick seemed to want the same distance she did and she should be glad. There was absolutely no reason to feel disappointed or frustrated. She had to cut this crap out.

Carrick's expression was implacable as he bent down to brush his lips across her cheekbone. She took the gesture for what it was, a polite thing to do, a small thanks-for-a-great-evening. It didn't mean anything more…couldn't mean a damn thing.

"I'll see you when I see you," he told her.

His cashmere coat was an expensive heap on the floor and he picked it up and pulled it on. He jammed his hand into the inside pocket and pulled out his phone. Then he winced.

"I've missed a dozen calls already. See you around, Sadie."

Sure. But not for a day or two. Or seven.

* * *

Sadie had five minutes to make her meeting in the conference room, a sleek, edgy room at the end of the hallway of the iconic, international and world-renowned auction house of Murphy International. It would only take thirty seconds to walk down the hallway, so she could hide out here in the bathroom for a little longer.

She'd do anything to avoid being alone with Carrick Murphy.

Sadie looked at her reflection in the mirror above the basin and rubbed a tiny speck of lipstick off her teeth. She'd spent the past week avoiding Carrick and, because they hadn't spent any time alone since the evening he'd stayed over, she knew he was avoiding her, too.

And that suited her just fine.

When she opened her door to Carrick hours after her near-death experience, she should've stripped the roses of their thorns instead of stripping the Murphy boss man of his clothes.

She wanted to blame her uncharacteristic behavior on seeing a white light or hearing angels sing except that she hadn't seen God or heard celestial choirs so that was a weak excuse.

Fact: Carrick Murphy was a great-looking man with a rocking body and she'd felt reckless and impulsive, desperate to celebrate being alive.

And, yep, doing Carrick Murphy, and having him do her, was exceedingly life-affirming. So were the multiple orgasms…

She couldn't be blamed for spending a few hours each night reliving that amazing evening, wishing he was with her again, touching her with those broad, long-fingered hands, kissing her with his sinful mouth.

But…

Like sailing to Antarctica on a tall ship, or catching the Orient Express, sex with Carrick was an indulgence, a once-in-a-lifetime experience.

Stunningly wonderful but never to be repeated.

Pity.

But she'd done this before and, as a result, knew that she had to slam her foot on the brakes. She'd fallen into the arms of a sexy man and, within a few weeks, fallen in love. She'd wanted to believe that Dennis was a good man, a man worth marrying.

Five years later, a marriage and ugly divorce later, she was stronger and wiser and fully understood that the same man who made you quiver and sigh could also make you cry. A pretty face could easily hide a cold heart, and malice could live under a charming facade.

Dennis had a lovely face and buckets of charm but under it all, he had the personality of a psychopathic honey badger. And from what she'd heard from Carrick's ex-wife and Beth, one of Sadie's oldest friends and her virtual assistant, so did Carrick.

Sadie hadn't been believed when she tried to tell her friends and family that Dennis was verbally abusing her and subjecting her to emotional torture that was both cruel and cunning. So when women she respected talked about their men, she listened.

But damn, why was she a magnet for bad boys?

And she wasn't talking about those cute, trouble-finds-me-but-I'm-a-good-guy-at-heart men. One of those she could handle. No, Sadie was attracted to *bad* bad boys. The ones who played games, lied, used…

Abused.

As had happened with her ex, nobody would suspect Carrick Murphy—a business phenomenon and a hell of an operator in the art world—of being a dick, but she'd heard enough from Tamlyn via Beth to understand that women should go into any relationship with him with their eyes propped open.

Not that that was what she was doing.

Sadie glanced at her watch again and, after readjusting her bag on her shoulder, she headed out, her heels clicking against the tiled floors. This was the first time she would be meeting Carrick's important clients and she wished she could definitively tell them that the painting was a lost Homer.

Not only because that news would set the art world alight—authenticating a "sleeper," a previously undiscovered painting, would be a kickass star on her résumé—but also because her job would then be over and she could remove herself from the temptation that was Carrick Murphy.

But she was many weeks, possibly months, away from submitting her final report. There was still so much data outstanding, including the results of the paint analysis. She was tracking down leads with regard to the labels on the back of the painting and she'd yet to receive any replies from the many galleries where Isabel and her family routinely bought art.

Establishing an artwork's authenticity took time. Sadie hoped Carrick's clients understood this.

Reaching the door to the conference room, Sadie lightly knocked and stepped inside. Because she was currently enjoying the luck of a blind mouse in a cattery, the room was empty except for Carrick, who stood by the large window, looking down onto Boston Common. He turned, that lethal smile flashing, hinting at that shallow dimple in his left cheek, and Sadie's heart kicked up a beat. Yep, there went her blood to that special place low in her womb, and heat meandered through her body.

Chemistry was a hell of a thing.

"Sadie."

Her name, rumbling out of Carrick's mouth, had never sounded sexier. Sadie sighed and just managed to stop herself from putting her hand on her heart.

Pulling her eyes off him, she placed her bag and her folders on the conference table and managed a quiet "good morning."

"Isabel's heirs are running late. They should be here in fifteen minutes or so."

Damn. What would they talk about while they waited? The weather? The painting? How amazing, strong, powerful and masculine he felt when he slid inside her...

Slade! So not helpful!

Thinking that she had to aim for sophistication or, at least, to act her age, Sadie walked over to the window, keeping a healthy distance between her and Carrick. Because, you know, chemistry…

Sadie saw him cast a glance over her outfit as she walked across the room and wondered if her boldly patterned red and orange dress was too arty and too bohemian for the conservative, upmarket offices of Murphy International.

She didn't care. She wasn't a black-suit-and-white-shirt-wearing type. She was an art lover and connoisseur, someone who needed color like other people needed to breathe. Carrick would get used to her clothes and if he didn't…

Tough.

She'd changed for one man, toned down her clothes, swallowed her thoughts and opinions and designed her life around a man who'd repaid her by having numerous affairs with everyone from her cousin to her masseuse. She would never dim her shine again, not for anyone.

Sadie looked past Carrick's very broad right shoulder to his stupendous view. The afternoon sun was starting to sink and the light held a touch of the same rose-pink Degas used for the dancers' tutus in his work *Dancers in Pink*. Or was it closer to the color of that rose Renoir painted in *Gabrielle à la Rose*?

Ooh, now she saw a hint of orange…

Carrick's knuckles rapping on the window brought her back to the present. She expected him to look annoyed, so his amusement was a surprise.

"Something happening on the common I should know about?"

Sadie took a moment to make sense of his words. She shook her head and waved at the window. "I have this habit of seeing colors in terms of art."

Confusion flashed in those grape-green eyes. "I don't understand."

Normally, she didn't try to explain, but for some inexplicable reason, she wanted Carrick to understand her obsession with color. Maybe if he did, they'd have something in common, a connection.

Something other than sex…

Seeing his interest, she looked down onto the busy street, trying to find an object to make her point. A woman cut across the common, wearing a yellow coat.

Sadie gripped Carrick's sleeve, her fingertips digging into the corded muscle of his forearm. She wanted to let go, but she could feel his heat, smell his clean, fresh skin.

"That woman, the one wearing yellow, do you see her?"

"Yeah."

Her fingers remained on his arm, as if stuck there with superglue. "Name the first painting that comes to mind where the artist used that color."

Carrick didn't hesitate. "Van Gogh's *Sunflowers*."

"Too easy. Try again."

"Andy Warhol's banana on the sleeve of The Velvet Underground's record?"

"Nope, try again," Sadie suggested.

"Jeez, you're tough." Carrick's brow furrowed in concentration. "Gustav Klimt's *Adele Bloch-Bauer*?"

Okay, that was a really good answer. "Better," she reluctantly admitted.

Carrick's laughter was low and rumbly. "Think you can do better?"

Please. "It reminds me of that untitled Mark Rothko work sold in New York a few years back." She cocked her head to the side. "Or maybe it's the color of *The Conspiracy of Claudius Civilis* by Rembrandt."

She felt Carrick's eyes on her profile, and she couldn't look at him, not sure if she wanted to see whether he was impressed or not.

"You know your art," Carrick said.

"I have a PhD in art history, so I should," Sadie replied, her tone crisp. Then she realized that she was stroking Carrick's arm like he was a cat with a particularly luxurious coat. She looked down at her hand, blushed and yanked it away.

"Sorry, along with color, I'm also a textile freak. And your suit is so soft, so…touchable."

Yeah, sure, the fabric was wonderfully soft, but that wasn't the real reason she was touching his arm.

Stop thinking about that night, Slade, and take your hand off his arm.

Sadie moved away from Carrick, folded her arms and hauled in a deep breath, telling herself to act like a professional.

Carrick stared down at the Common and they silently watched the Boston residents taking advantage of the cold, clear afternoon. After a minute of silence, Carrick pointed to a woman dressed in a fuchsia-

colored coat and walking two elegant, very well be-
haved Great Danes.

"The pink coat of the woman walking the Great
Danes is the same color as the floor in Matisse's *The
Pink Studio*," he said.

"Or the pink in O'Keeffe's *It Was Yellow and
Pink*."

They could talk about art, thank goodness. It was a
neutral subject, something they were both passionate
about. And far safer than their other mutual interest:
their fascination with each other's bodies.

"I also think it's the same color as your nipples
after I lave them with my tongue."

It took Sadie a few seconds for his words to sink
in and she flushed, immediately catapulted back to
that night and the shooting, aching ribbons of pleasure running through her, heating her from the inside
out. Sadie couldn't look at him; she knew that if she
did, if she saw the passion in his eyes, she'd fly into
his arms and curl herself around him.

Not exactly appropriate behavior for a conference
meeting. His clients might feel slightly in the way.

Sadie placed her hands on the glass and stared
down at the small cars and tiny people. The dog
walker was gone but the pedestrians below often
tipped their faces to the weak sun, enjoying the little
heat on offer.

"I haven't been able to stop thinking about that
night."

Sadie groaned and placed her forehead on the glass
between her hands. She couldn't stop thinking about

it, either, but she didn't want to admit that, didn't want
to continue this conversation because Carrick's ob-
servations both bemused and befuddled her.

The only thing she was sure of was that she couldn't
talk art and paintings and forensics while memories of
that night swirled around her overheated brain.

"Carrick, please stop talking about it."

Carrick moved closer, and Sadie could feel his
heat. "Why? Because you regret it or because talking about it makes you hot?"

This wasn't the behavior of a man intent on avoiding her. After he left and didn't call or text, she'd
assumed he considered her as just another casual
hookup and had moved on. His comments suggested
he wouldn't mind a repeat.

Neither, dammit, would she.

But that would be foolish and Sadie wasn't gen-
erally a foolish woman. Except she had totally lost
her head when she allowed Carrick Murphy to push
her up against the wall in her apartment and kiss her
senseless.

She could lie to herself and say she wished she
hadn't slept with him, but she couldn't force herself,
even mentally, to issue such a whopper. She didn't regret what they'd done, the hot evening they'd shared,
but she had to move on. Now, immediately.

But man, when she looked into those light green
eyes and saw his blatant desire, she felt foolish and
reckless. The urge to strip was strong.

Nope, not happening. "It's best if we just forget
about that night," Sadie said, pulling her hands off

the glass. She gripped her hands behind her back and stepped away to put a solid amount of space between her and Carrick.

"I don't think that is going to happen anytime soon," Carrick muttered, his deep voice rich with frustration. "I want you, Sadie. God, I know we shouldn't, that it's a crap idea, that we said it was a onetime thing, but then you walk into the room and all I can think about is being inside you as soon as possible. And judging by all that blue fire in your eyes, by the way they keep going to my mouth, racing over my body, I think you want that, too."

He was spot-on, dammit.

But you can't go there, you have to be sensible, Slade. "I also want to find out who modeled for Da Vinci in *La Belle Ferronnière*. I want to own one of Manet's bride paintings, find the Russian amber room. But I'm a realist and I know that none of the above will happen, just like I know that a repeat of that night is a solidly bad idea."

Also, because the last time I was this attracted, I ended up marrying the guy and he made my life hell.

Carrick, so she was told, was cut from the same cloth. Initially charming and attentive and then turning into a monster at the first hint of something deeper.

"Screw good ideas. They aren't any fun," Carrick muttered, jamming his hands in the pockets of his suit pants, pulling back his jacket to reveal his broad chest covered by a mint-green shirt.

His suit was designer—maybe Armani?—his tie

Hermès and perfectly knotted. To anyone else, he looked like a ridiculously successful Boston businessman, but Sadie was beginning to see past the implacable facade he presented the world. Beneath his layer of perpetual cool, red-hot lava churned.

And damn, those contrasts, seeing the passion beneath the surface, made her hot. And horny.

What could happen if she spent one more night with him? Except that one night probably wouldn't be enough and, in another week, maybe two, they'd be back in the same position again, yearning and burning.

Nope, it was better to be resolute now, to nip this in the bud.

Sadie opened her mouth to say no, fully intending to tell him there wasn't the slightest chance that they'd hook up again.

"I'll think about it."

Sadie almost turned around, convinced that some other woman had uttered the words she'd never meant to say. Or maybe she'd imagined saying them, but then she looked at Carrick's face and saw the flash of excitement in his eyes, the twitch of pleased lips. Oh, crap.

What in the world was wrong with her and since when did her mouth act independently of her brain?

Carrick cupped her cheek with his hand and placed his lips on her temple. Sadie forced herself to keep her hands at her sides, bunching her fists so she didn't grip his hips, run her hands up that wide chest.

"Think hard. And think quick," Carrick murmured.

Two

Carrick stepped away, buttoned his suit jacket and moved to the door of the conference room. He pulled it wide and stood aside to allow two women to enter the room. Sadie watched as the small blonde returned Carrick's hug, conscious of the streaks of jealousy coursing through her body. Annoyed with herself—there was nothing to be jealous about; she and Carrick had shared their bodies, not their souls—she turned her attention onto the second woman casually dressed in black.

The woman was of Indian descent; Sadie could see that in her lovely, light brown skin and the shape of her luminous gray eyes. They were, Sadie decided, eyes that would change with her mood or with the color of her clothes, the gray-blue of Sisley's fog or the green-gray of a Whistler sea. Her nose was perfectly straight and her cheekbones could cut glass.

Man, she was gorgeous.

Carrick ushered the women into the room and gestured to Sadie. "Keely, Joa, meet Dr. Sadie Slade. She's the art detective we've employed to work on your painting. Sadie, Keely Mounton and Joa Jones."

"Hi, Sadie, nice to meet you," Keely—the blonde—said, shaking Sadie's hand. She looked at Carrick, her smile small but infectious. "And it's Ju-ah, not Jo-ah." Keely dropped her bag on the conference table as Sadie and Joa shook hands. "She never corrects anyone, but I know it drives her mad when people mispronounce her name."

"I am standing right here, Keels," Joa replied with a wry smile. "Sorry, Keely has been bossing me around for half my life and I don't see her stopping anytime soon."

Joa's smile took her from stunning to exquisite. Sadie darted a glance at Carrick, expecting his tongue to be on the floor, but his expression was inscrutable and he looked completely unaffected.

Well...*huh.*

After exchanging small talk—mutual acquaintances and the horrible winter weather—Carrick gestured for them to take a seat. When they did, Sadie took the seat opposite his clients.

Sliding his hands into the pockets of his suit pants, Carrick looked every inch the corporate CEO of an international company. "Sadie, Isabel Mounton-Matthews was a valued and important client of Murphy's. I think she bought her first painting from us over forty years ago. She and my stepmom, Raeni, were great friends and she passed away about—" he raised his eyebrows at Keely "—a year ago?"

Keely nodded. "Fourteen months to be precise."

"Keely and Joa jointly inherited her estate," Carrick continued.

Lucky, lucky girls. Gorgeous and wealthy and now owners of one of the best art collections in the country.

"Keely and Joa have decided to sell the bulk of the collection through Murphy International and donate the proceeds to Isabel's foundation, which supports various charities on the east coast. Her collection will be the sale of the decade. If you want a comparison, think of the Rockefeller collection that was sold a few years back. Isabel's collection more than competes. She collected masterpieces, porcelain, jewelry, Native American art, Asian art, silver, furniture, textiles."

"My aunt was a magpie with a lot of money," Keely cheerfully agreed.

"My brother Finn is cataloging the collection, which is extensive, but he doesn't have time to delve into the mystery of your paintings, ladies. And that's why I hired Sadie," Carrick said. "And Sadie has already determined that two of the three paintings are Homer copies."

Keely pulled a face and Joa sighed. "I'm not that surprised. I'm sure I recall Iz mentioning that she wasn't fully convinced they were all by Homer. She had a gut instinct for art and a fabulous eye. And pedigree wasn't important to her, she liked what she liked," Keely said, resting her forearms on the table. She turned to Sadie. "So what makes you think the two paintings are copies?"

Carrick looked at Sadie, and she explained. "While the paintings are by an artist with talent, the execution simply isn't good enough to be a Homer. They lack his energy and verve. The signature is wrong and the colors are off. They simply aren't accomplished enough to be a Winslow Homer. But the third painting is exceptional."

"Are we talking about the one that's unsigned?" Joa quietly asked. When Sadie nodded, Joa continued. "If it is by Homer, shouldn't it be signed? Isn't that what artists do?"

"Not necessarily. There are lots of reasons an artist didn't sign their works. Sometimes they thought the work wasn't good enough. Sometimes they never completed it. Sometimes they simply forgot." Sadie divided her glance between Keely and Joa. "How emotionally invested are you in this being a Homer?"

A small frown pulled Keely's dark eyebrows together and those deep brown eyes reflected her confusion. "I'm not sure what you mean?"

"Was the painting one of your aunt's favorites? Is it a favorite of yours? How disappointed will you be if it's not a Homer?"

Keely exchanged a quick look with Joa, who simply shrugged. Keely answered her question.

"The unsigned painting always hung in the small sitting room at Mounton House, adjacent to what was

Isabel's bedroom. All her favorite paintings hung there so I know she liked it. She obviously had her doubts about the other two because I found them in her cupboard in her bedroom when I was up there doing inventory with Mr. Snooty Pants—" Keely glared at Joa "—and you owe me for doing that, by the way."

"Mr. Snooty Pants?" Joa asked, puzzled.

"Wilfred Seymour." Keely uttered the name as if poor Wilfred was an all-powerful wizard who shouldn't be named.

"Are you talking about Dare?" Carrick asked. When Keely nodded, he released a low chuckle.

"He's the least snooty guy I know," Carrick stated.

Sadie didn't know Keely, but she instantly recognized the woman's stubborn expression. Possibly because she'd seen it on her own face a time or two.

"I have, obviously, seen a totally different version of the man than you have."

"He's a pretty cool guy, Keely," Carrick protested. Points to Carrick for defending his friend, Sadie thought.

"We'll have to agree to disagree on that subject," Keely retorted. Sadie met Joa's eyes and caught her small smile. Yep, she knew what Joa was thinking because Sadie was thinking it, too…something along the lines of the lady and protesting too much.

"Moving on from annoying lawyers…" Keely waved away the subject of Dare Seymour.

Sadie sympathized. It was exceedingly annoying

to be attracted to a man you didn't want to be, or couldn't afford to be, attracted to.

Joa pulled them back to the subject at hand. "Just to be clear, we are talking about the painting of the African American woman with her two children in the fields, right?"

Sadie nodded. "Let me explain…"

Sadie pulled her iPad toward her and flipped open the cover. Powering up the device, she waited until it connected with the big screen behind Carrick. When the painting appeared on the screen, Carrick moved to sit next to her so his bulk didn't block their view. He immediately pressed his knee against hers and Sadie lost her train of thought.

Sadie knew they were waiting for her to speak, to tell them how she spent her very expensive time— time they were paying for—but nope…

Her brain had ceased to function. Ground to a halt. No blood flowing.

Mostly because she was remembering the way Carrick spread her knees open, the way he looked at the most intimate parts of her, his expression as he dipped his head…

Complete shutdown…

Sadie jumped when Carrick filled the increasingly awkward silence. "So Sadie is going to take you through what she's found and you'll both have a better idea of what we are facing."

Sadie gave herself a mental slap, told herself to get with the program and do her job. But just to minimize distractions, she stood up and moved away from Murphy and his addictive touch.

"So, you'll contact me as soon as you have some news?"

"Because I'm contracted to Murphy's, I report to them, but if Carrick is happy for me to liaise with you directly, I'm happy to do that."

"I have no problem with Sadie doing that, Keely."

Carrick Murphy's deep voice drifted over to Joa, who stood in the hallway outside the conference room. She mentally urged Keely to hurry up. Joa loved her best friend and non-blood sister but damn, she never stopped talking. Joa had come directly from the airport to this meeting and she was jetlagged, tired and hungry. Keely had promised to whisk her back to Mounton House as soon as possible.

Joa swallowed down a huge yawn, thinking that she instinctively liked Sadie and appreciated her professional, shoot-from-the-hip approach. She wouldn't make them any false promises or raise their hopes unnecessarily. Joa, who was above everything else a wide-eyed realist, appreciated that.

Joa rocked on her feet, feeling, like she often did, that this, her life, was all a dream. She was still unable, so many months after Isabel's death, to believe that she was a beneficiary of Isabel's great fortune.

The fortune comprised of a historic house in Boston's Back Bay neighborhood, a stupendously healthy stock portfolio, various bank accounts and one of the best art collections in the world.

Windfalls—a tame word for such an enormous inheritance—didn't happen to people like her.

It was right for Keely to inherit; she was a blood relation of Isabel's. But Joa had no such connections to the Mounton-Matthews family. She'd only met Isabel at fourteen when the Boston doyenne visited a shelter that had been a stopgap after Joa ran away from her latest foster home.

The very next day Joa had found herself living at Mounton House with the eccentric Isabel and her great-niece Keely. For the first time since she was shoved into the system at ten, Joa had felt loved. But better than loved, she'd felt secure.

Safety. So many people took the concept for granted, but to Joa, there wasn't any better feeling in the world. And she'd always be eternally grateful to Isabel for making her feel that way.

Man, she missed the old lady with an intensity that threatened to drop her to her knees.

"Are you sure Isabel didn't say anything to you about where she acquired the paintings?" Sadie asked Keely.

Right, Joa would have to wait a little longer for her bed.

"Not that I recall," Keely answered. "Maybe she didn't buy them. Maybe they were given to her. Iz was exceptionally popular and had many…friends."

Why didn't Keely just come straight out and say that Iz had numerous lovers over the years? Joa doubted Sadie would fall over in a heap upon hearing that Iz liked men. And sex.

"Ah, got it. Any idea who she was seeing when she received the paintings?"

"It was way before my time," Keely replied. "Her diaries talk about her visitors—" Joa rolled her eyes at the euphemism "—but she doesn't name names."

Mainly because Isabel had affairs with very prominent men and they would not be happy if their liaisons were exposed. Their wives wouldn't be too thrilled, either.

"Damn. I might've been able to trace a sale through a name," Sadie said. "Are we talking the cream of Boston society?"

"Yep," Keely cheerfully replied. "She was universally adored, on both sides of the Atlantic. She was as popular in London and Paris as she was in Boston."

Keely so easily spoke of people in Isabel's milieu, high-society Boston. Keely had stepped into her grandaunt's shoes rather well in that respect. Joa had no interest in spending time in that rarefied society.

She never felt more like a runaway, like a girl from the wrong side of the tracks, than when she was faced with people with more money than God and a pedigree they could trace back to the Mayflower. No thanks; she'd stay in the shadows where she felt most comfortable.

This wasn't her world; these weren't her people. Well, Keely was, obviously. Though Joa had to admit that Sadie Slade seemed rather nice and, more important, very down-to-earth.

And if Joa wasn't wrong, and she seldom was,

Sadie and Carrick Murphy had something hot and sexy happening.

Lucky girl, because the guy was super-fine.

Joa walked down the hallway to look at a collection of old photographs on the wall opposite, smiling at a photo of three teenage boys crowding a much younger girl. She knew enough about Boston society to identify the Murphy brothers and their sister Tanna.

They looked like a happy family and, while Joa was sorry their parents were dead, she thought the siblings lucky to have had the experience of being part of a supportive and close family.

Some people, her included, had never had that experience.

Joa heard masculine footsteps and turned to watch a tall man with unruly brown hair, heavy stubble and tired eyes walking down the hallway toward her. Her heart bounced around her chest as she clocked the real-life version of the man she'd briefly seen when Keely Facetimed him shortly before their meeting.

The real-life version of the face on her sister's phone was spectacular. His open-collared chambray shirt revealed a chest that was lightly covered with hair. The shirt was tucked into a pair of olive-green khaki pants, showing off long, muscular legs. Joa lifted her eyes to examine that fallen angel face and instantly clocked his resemblance to Carrick, in the color of his eyes and in that straight nose and a stubborn chin. Carrick, in his designer suit and perfectly knotted tie, looked more corporate, more buttoned-down, than this Murphy with his funky watch and leather bangles around a strong wrist.

Hottie alert, Joa decided, idly noting that the butterflies in her stomach were beating their wings in excitement. And appreciation. When had she last had such a visceral, sexual reaction to a man? Last year? Two years ago?

Never might be closer to the truth.

Joa stood to one side of the hall, wondering if he'd take his eyes off his iPad long enough to notice her or if he'd just walk straight past.

Ronan Murphy, lost in his own world, walked straight past her.

Joa wasn't crazy about attention, but even she wouldn't mind being noticed by a hot, hot, hot man.

Joa watched that broad back and that spectacular ass walk away, very appreciative of the view. Ronan was about to turn the corner when Keely flew out of the conference room and hollered for him to stop. Ronan spun around, grinned at Keely and hurried back down the passageway to where she stood, hands on her hips.

"Morning, Keels." His voice was as deep as Carrick's, but Ronan's was touched by gravel and had a sexy rasp that sent chills racing over Joa's skin. "How goes the authentication process?"

Keely pouted. "Slowly." Without turning around, Keely reached back, grabbed the sleeve of Joa's coat and tugged her forward. "I've been dying for you two to meet. Ro, this is Joa."

Joa expected him to hand her a perfunctory greeting before turning his attention back to Keely, but his eyes collided with hers. Yes, his eyes were green but that was lazy thinking. They were green touched with gold, copper and shocking blue. They held all the colors of a fantastic abalone shell.

She could spend hours, days, months, looking into those eyes, reading their secrets. Because, boy, this man sure did have a lot.

As did she.

Ronan smiled, his sexy mouth lifting at the corners, but that practiced smile didn't reach his eyes. "Hello, Joa. Keely mentioned you were on your way home. Are you happy to be back in Boston?"

"I am, thank you."

Joa tipped her head to the side as she held his gaze. Cute, smart and very practiced at pulling out this urbane, charming side. She wondered what he was like beneath all that slick.

Keely interrupted her musings and their eye lock. "I'm so glad I caught you, Ronan. Have you found a nanny for your boys yet?"

"No."

Keely grinned at him. "Good. That makes this a lot easier."

"Makes what easier?"

Joa didn't know what she was talking about, either. "Ro, Joa has been working as an au pair for years and she is going to be your new nanny. She needs something to do while figuring out the next phase of her life, so she might as well look after the monsters while she muses."

What. The. Hell?

* * *

Sadie watched Keely fly out of the room, bemused by the blonde's whirlwind approach to life. Sadie placed her reports back into their folder, conscious of Carrick looking at her from across the room. He stood by the top-of-the-line coffee machine, his eyes on her face as he waited for the machine to fill his cup.

"Can I make you a cup of coffee, Sadie?"

Sadie closed the lid to her laptop and shook her head. She'd far prefer a cup of chamomile tea to settle her jittery stomach. Work was easy—being around Carrick made her jumpy. "I'm fine, thank you."

Such a lie...

Carrick picked up his cup and walked over to the open door, kicking it closed and shutting off the conversation happening outside. Providing them with privacy. She didn't want privacy and she didn't want to be alone with Carrick because she couldn't guarantee that she'd still be clothed at the end of their conversation.

Her lack of self-control around this man was ridiculous. Yeah, he was hot, but so was a volcano and both were equally dangerous. Why, oh, why couldn't she be attracted to calm, nice, reasonably good-looking guys who didn't ooze charisma and sex appeal? Why was she only ever attracted to alpha men with no shortage of good looks and confidence?

And a strong streak of jerk?

Carrick placed his cup on the conference table and perched on the edge next to her, long legs stretched, crossed at the ankles.

"Are you done thinking and can I buy you dinner tonight?"

His out-of-the-blue question had Sadie jerking her head up, her eyes narrowing. What was he playing at?

Carrick raising the subject of them sleeping together again didn't surprise her, but his offer of dinner did. Dinner implied that he wanted to spend time out of the bedroom with her and that simply wasn't happening. Talking, laughing, getting to know each other was out of the question.

Even if Carrick wasn't too like her ex for comfort, she wasn't interested in dating. Dating—dinner, coffee, drinks, no matter what form it took—was invented to get to know someone better and she wasn't interested. What was the point when she wasn't prepared to start another relationship?

"Carrick, I think it's better if we keep our relationship professional," Sadie said, resting her hand on her closed laptop and her other fist on her hip.

"I think that horse bolted," Carrick replied. He lifted one shoulder in an "aw shucks" shrug. Then he smiled that crooked, sexy smile and she narrowed her eyes. Yeah, she wasn't going to fall under his I'm-so-sexy-I'm-difficult-to-resist spell again.

"First, we've already slept together so you don't need to buy me dinner."

Carrick stood up, and when his eyes hit hers, she saw his annoyance. "What do you mean by that?"

Sadie met his annoyance with defiance. "You want to sleep with me again—you've told me that. You don't need to spin the whole dinner line."

Carrick's expression turned colder and his eyes were touched with frost. "Wow. What is your problem?"

Sadie pushed a finger into his chest. "You. And men like you. You're not being honest and I hate that."

Carrick stood up and pushed his hands into the pockets of his suit pants. Sadie thought he looked an inch or two taller, slightly broader, than just a few moments before. He was properly angry and Sadie wondered why she wasn't feeling scared. Had this been Dennis, she would be finding a way to placate him, to distract him, to divert the incoming river of vitriol and verbal abuse.

But with Carrick, she didn't feel anxious or scared. Not even a little.

Huh.

But just in case she was wrong about Carrick, in case her radar was faulty, Sadie steeled herself. Men like Dennis and Carrick didn't take rejection well.

Sadie straightened her spine, lifted her chin and squared her shoulders. No matter what Carrick said, she wouldn't let him hurt her. She'd been hurt enough for too long by a stupid, thoughtless man. She refused to let Carrick exert the same power over her.

The rogue thought crossed her mind that, if she lowered her guard, Carrick Murphy could slice and dice her into smaller pieces than Dennis ever managed. But she wouldn't let that happen; she categorically refused.

When Carrick placed his hands on her shoulders, Sadie stiffened. Oh, not because she feared him, but because she really, really wanted to bury her nose in his neck, to wind her arms around his back and hold on.

She was an independent, capable woman, but even strong women sometimes needed to lean.

Carrick Murphy was not, she reminded herself, lean-able.

"Who the hell hurt you, Sadie?" Carrick murmured, his words like a caress. "And tell me where I can find him so I can rearrange his face."

Sadie almost smiled at the image of Carrick pounding Dennis to a pulp. But as nice as that picture was, she was responsible for her own actions and marrying a smooth-talking, seemingly charming man who was as charismatic as hell had been her decision and she lived with that choice.

She'd thought Dennis was her white knight, her Prince Charming, but he'd turned out to be ugly and manipulative. He'd taught her that the prettiest packaging could conceal the blackest soul.

Carrick might be temptation personified, but she wouldn't make that mistake again. Sadie pulled away and picked up her laptop to put it inside her tote bag, but Carrick's hand on hers had her turning to face him.

She forced herself to lift her eyebrows, to keep her face inscrutable.

"You can try to look unaffected, but I can feel your pulse hammering beneath my fingertips," Carrick told her, his thumb drifting over the pulse point on the inside of her wrist.

It was time to end this, to put to rest their very brief fling. "No to dinner, Carrick. No to sex. We're business colleagues, that's all. The other night didn't happen."

"But it did."

"Then we should pretend that it didn't!" Sadie retorted, pulling her wrist from his grip.

"As much as I would love a magic wand that clears our mind of inconvenient memories, life doesn't work that way. And I don't mind the memories of that night. They are, after all, scorching hot," Carrick stated. "Earlier you said I wasn't being honest. Do you want me to be honest, Sadie? Can you handle my honesty?"

Of course she could. Well, she thought she could. Maybe. But she was, judging by Carrick's serious face, about to find out.

"I think you are fascinating, possibly the most intriguing woman I've ever met." Carrick's deep voice filled the space between them. "I spend my nights reliving that night, the memory of you."

Sadie felt her cheeks flame.

"I can be even more honest… I want you, in my bed, under me, my mouth on yours as I slide into you. I want to hear your screams as I make you come and I want to feel your hair on my stomach as you take me between your lips."

His graphic words created a buzz low in her womb and she felt her heart rate spike. Sadie wondered if he could feel it in her pulse and, judging by the pressure from his fingers and that small, satisfied smile, he could.

"So yeah, maybe I did offer to take you to dinner in the hope that it would lead to another night, but I don't think a couple hours talking would do any harm. We have a lot in common and I wouldn't mind spending time dancing around your mind before taking you to bed again."

"Why?" Sadie asked him. "What's the point?"

A frown pulled Carrick's eyebrows together and he dropped her wrist. "Does there have to be a point?"

"Dinner equals a date and dating implies that you are looking for something more than sex," Sadie pointed out. "Just so we are clear, I'm not interested in a relationship. I have no intention of investing my time and energy into a man only to be disappointed again. I did that once and I am not stupid enough to do that again."

Carrick handed her a deep frown. "You really need to tell me who did a number on your head."

That wasn't ever going to happen. She'd discussed her marriage with numerous people, including her family, and nobody had believed her. Why would they believe her when everyone knew what an awesome guy her ex was, how lucky she was to have married him? How stupid she'd been to divorce him…

Carrick folded his arms across his chest, and his big biceps pulled his shirtsleeves tight. "I'm just offering to feed you, Slade, and to make you scream. I'm not offering to marry you or asking you to have my babies. I think you are overreacting…"

She could understand why he felt like that. Sadie pulled her bottom lip between her teeth, looking for a way to tell him that she knew more about his marriage than she should, that she knew how he'd treated Tamlyn. But she couldn't say anything, partly because this situation was complicated enough already without him knowing that her virtual assistant was also his ex-sister-in-law.

It was time to end this conversation, right now.

"Carrick, I'm attracted to you. I would never have slept with you if I wasn't. But I am wise enough to sense that you are—" she hesitated, pulling back the *dangerous* that hovered on her lips "—complicated. I don't do complicated."

She frowned at him, and, feeling a little vulnerable, decided to go on the offensive. "I thought we agreed not to discuss this again?"

"I know, we did say that but—" Carrick raked his fingers through his hair "—but I can't stop thinking about how good we were together! And I suspect you feel the same way."

She did. Dammit.

Sadie gripped the bridge of her nose.

She desperately wanted to stamp her foot or kick his shins but only because he was right. They were good together. But good sex didn't equate to his being a good man...

End this. Now.

Sadie nailed him with an *I'm done* look, knowing she had to shut down this conversation before she succumbed to temptation and asked him to take her on this sturdy boardroom table.

He wouldn't say no...

Be sensible, Slade.

"Having a one-night stand is not something I indulge in and I'm not into short-term flings. Or, as I said, long-term relationships."

Leaving her in no-sex land. Well, how sad, too bad.

Sadie squared her shoulders and forced the words past her lips. "Either we forget what happened the other night or I walk out and you find another art appraiser. I'm not going to have this discussion again."

She *had* to protect herself; it was the only sensible course of action.

Carrick's green eyes narrowed. "Are you sure that's what you want?"

No, but she'd never admit that. It took all she had to give him a quick, jerky nod. Carrick held her stare, his expression now inscrutable. "Fine. I won't mention it again."

Okay, then.

It—they—were over and she'd gotten what she'd asked for. So why then did she feel so disappointed? Why did she still want him to pull her to his hard body, lower his mouth to cover hers? Why did she still want him?

Because apparently, she was still, when it came to men, a complete idiot.

Sadie wrapped her arms around her body and watched him stride from the room, his big body radiating tension. She wanted to run after him and to stop herself, she gripped the desk and locked her knees.

They'd only shared one night of great sex and it

was completely pointless to think they had the potential to be anything more to each other than a hot, sexy memory.

It's done, Slade; it's over.

After rolling her head to relieve some of the knots in her neck, Sadie pulled her bag onto her shoulder.

She had a job to do, and to do it effectively she'd have to evade and avoid the boss man. Good thing she'd had some practice at doing exactly that over the past week.

Three

Carrick slammed the weights back into the rack and grabbed his towel, roughly swiping it over his sweaty face. He glanced at the oversize clock on the wall. He still had fifteen minutes left and he needed to get his heart rate up, to feel it pounding out of his chest.

Anything to dislodge the dull ache he currently lived with. Had it only been yesterday since his "thanks, but no thanks" conversation with Sadie?

Stepping onto the treadmill, he pushed buttons, looking for a high-intensity program. As the belt moved, he started to run. He would not think about Sadie, nor did he want to think about how much her rejection of him, correction, her *rejection of sex*, hurt. But as much as he didn't want to think about her, he couldn't damn well stop.

And thinking about rejection made him think about his marriage and that just sucked. It was a topic he seldom visited, preferring to leave that monumental stuff up in the past.

His story wasn't that unusual or uncommon: he'd married in a haze of sex, fell out of love and wanted out of the marriage. He'd tried to keep things amicable, respectful. But Tam didn't take rejection well and when she found out she couldn't change his mind, she'd opted to punish him instead.

Had Sadie heard the false rumors about his marriage? Probably. Might Sadie be avoiding him, and his bed, because of Tamlyn? The world they operated in was a small one and filled with misinformed, malicious gossips.

It was a distinct possibility.

The urge to tell Sadie his side of the story was strong, but he immediately squashed that idea. His pride, ever vigilant, refused to allow him to explain a damn thing.

And he couldn't forget that he didn't know Sadie well enough, or trust her enough, to expose himself. Despite years passing, he was still embarrassed that he'd been, probably still was, talked about. Having his private life and his marriage play out in the court of public opinion had been a nasty experience, and the memories still left a bitter taste in his mouth.

Grown-ups, those with any thought processes at all, knew there were two sides to a story, his and hers. Or, more accurately, his, hers and the truth. Tamlyn had some valid complaints. He had spent far too much time at the office and he had avoided going home.

But he'd never cheated on her or verbally abused Tamlyn. In fact, instead of talking to her, he'd mentally and physically withdrawn, and to someone who craved attention, that was the cruelest punishment of all. He wasn't proud of himself. He probably could've handled the whole asking-for-a-divorce conversation better, but Tamlyn turned...yeah, vicious.

Tamlyn, he thought again, didn't take rejection well. And judging by his pissy mood, neither, apparently, did he.

He'd decided, sometime during his separation from Tamlyn, not to try and combat the swirl of rumors surrounding their relationship. What other people thought wasn't important enough to rent space in his head. He didn't care what strangers thought about him; the people he loved and cared about knew the truth. So damned if he would explain. And he refused to break that policy with Sadie.

While it annoyed and frustrated him that Sadie might believe he was the bad guy Tamlyn made him out to be, Sadie was a temporary distraction in his life and not important enough to him to explain that very ugly period of his life.

Or, that was what he was trying to believe.

There was no point in raking up the past. There was no chance of them taking whatever they had up a level; she wasn't interested in a relationship and neither was he. And if that was true—and he was sure it was—then why had he suggested dinner? Why had he told her he wanted to dance through her mind?

Dance.

Through her mind.

What the hell, Murphy?

But he couldn't deny that she was an interesting woman; he liked the way her mind worked. Underneath the colorful clothes and perfect face was a razor-sharp mind. He liked interesting people and if an interesting discussion led to fantastic sex, who was he to complain?

His liking her mind, her spirit, did not mean that he'd ever think about commitment, love, putting a ring on her finger. That was just stupid...

And he was just as stupid, spending so much time thinking about Dr. Sadie Slade. What he needed to do was find another woman to drive her out of his mind...

Carrick hit the button to speed up and pumped his arms and lengthened his stride, his breathing now ragged. He lifted his hand to wipe the sweat out of his eyes and out of the corner of his eye saw a big hand punching the stop button on the console. The belt slowed and Carrick scowled at Ronan.

"Problem?" Carrick asked between breaths.

"Well, yeah, since I've called your name three times and you didn't hear me," Ronan replied. He tipped his head to the side. "Everything okay?"

Carrick flashed a smile at his younger-by-a-year brother. He wanted to bitch, but he felt uncomfortable talking about women when his brother was still missing his gorgeous wife. The Murphy boys didn't have great luck at relationships, Carrick and Finn were both divorced and Ro was a young widower.

Great luck? Hell, they didn't have any luck at all.

"I'm good."

"Really?" Ronan looked skeptical. "Because you were mumbling to yourself and you powered through your workout like a demon, a sure sign something is worrying you."

Ronan knew him too well. "Nah, I'm good."

"Liar," Ronan countered as Carrick stepped off the treadmill. "This wouldn't have something to do with Sadie Slade, would it?"

Carrick hid his surprised expression behind his towel. He made a show of wiping his face and only dropped the towel when he was certain his expression was inscrutable. "Why would you think that?"

Ronan lifted his dark eyebrows. "Oh, the fact that you turned pea-green and were scared out of your mind when she choked at the pre-exhibition cocktail party."

They'd been some of the worst minutes of his life, but he wasn't going to admit that to his brother. Carrick handed Ronan a that's-all-you-got? look. "She's consulting for us and she choked on food served at a *Murphy* event."

Ronan ignored his explanation. "And every time you two are together, the room crackles with electricity."

"Crap," Carrick replied before turning his back to Ronan to head for the water dispenser. He filled a cup, downed the water and filled the cup again. Not wanting to discuss Sadie—he'd given that frustrating woman far too much of his time as it was—he changed the subject. "Have you found a nanny yet?"

"Keely suggested that Joa help me out. She's an au pair and she's got time on her hands." Ronan looked uncomfortable and Carrick's big-brother radar beeped. "You met her the other day, didn't you?"

"Yeah." Carrick nodded.

"What did you think about her?" Ronan asked.

Why were they talking about Joa? Carrick had no idea, but as long as they weren't discussing Sadie, he'd go with it. "She seemed pleasant. Gorgeous as hell, obviously, but smart. She asked some pertinent questions about art and the Homer in particular. Are you going to hire her?"

Ronan shifted and shrugged. "Dunno."

Carrick knew Ronan desperately needed a nanny. Joa was available, had experience and Keely recommended her. Why wasn't Ronan jumping all over this?

Could it be because Ronan was finally starting to notice women again? It worried Carrick that Ronan had shown no interest in women, or sex, since Thandi's death. Sex was a biological function, something men in their thirties needed. He'd raised the subject with Ronan and had been told to back off, that sex was a momentary release and it certainly did not have the power to penetrate grief.

He'd backed off.

But Ronan's questions about Joa gave Carrick hope. To the world, his brother was the funny, fast-talking Murphy, able to charm birds from the trees, but Carrick had held him as he cried, watched over him and his kids as he drank himself into oblivion those first few weeks after Thandi passed away.

Ronan had regained his charm, but it was all surface; underneath he was still broken and battered.

"Are you hesitant about hiring her because she's stunning?" Carrick asked, looking for some sort of agreement in Ronan's eyes, and there it was, a flicker of acknowledgment and was that...possessiveness? Better and better...

"Or because she is smart and sexy?" Carrick knew he was pushing Ronan's patience, but thought it was worth it. "Don't you think?"

Ronan shrugged. "I guess. Not that I can look at her like that."

Carrick sighed. In Ronan's head, having a relationship with anyone would be cheating on Thandi, and while his brother was a rabble-rouser and a party animal—or he had been—he did not cheat.

None of them did.

"Ro, you're allowed to be attracted to someone other than Thandi," Carrick quietly told him.

Ronan's stark gaze met his. "Whether I am or not is beside the point. We don't fool around with our employees, Carrick. It's a recipe for disaster and you, of all people, know that."

Ouch. Carrick sighed. "Sadie and I just had one night, Ronan. And it's over."

Surprise jumped into Ronan's eyes. "Ah, well, okay. And more than I needed to know about you and Sadie. Actually, I was referring to Satan's bride, Tamlyn. You met her when you worked together on restoring that Kahlo."

Carrick winced. Crap. He was so busted. Looking for a way out, he picked up on Ronan's previous sentence. "At the risk of sounding reasonable, may I point out that hiring Joa as your nanny might be the answer to all your problems?"

"Or the source of a dozen more," Ronan muttered, walking away.

Carrick watched Ronan as he headed to the rowing machine and winced. Yep, just another stunning woman causing chaos in a Murphy male's life. On the plus side, Carrick was grateful he wasn't alone.

Misery, after all, liked company.

That evening, Joa was still irritated with Keely but that didn't stop her from taking the glass of red wine Keely waved under her nose. She was still mad at her foster sister for being so damn high-handed, for volunteering Joa to be the very sexy Ronan Murphy's nanny…

Keely had always been as bossy as hell, but they were adults now and she had no right to interfere in Joa's life.

So if that was the case, why hadn't she flat-out refused?

Keely dropped into the corner of the sofa in the library of Mounton House and put her feet on the coffee table, her sock-covered toes pointing in the direction of the wood fire crackling in the elaborate fireplace. "God, it's cold out there."

Joa, knowing that Keely hated the silent treatment, didn't reply.

"So what are your impressions of Sadie Slade?"

So they were going to dance around the subject. Okay, then. "She seems professional and smart. I have no doubt she will find the answers we need."

"If that painting is a Homer, it will raise an enormous amount for the foundation." Keely rested her head on the back of the sofa, a small smile on her face. "I've known Carrick and his brothers for a long time, but I've never seen Carrick so distracted before."

Joa wasn't going to ask; she was still mad at Keely...

"What do you mean?"

Such willpower, Joa.

Keely's mouth twitched at Joa's curiosity. "Carrick couldn't keep his eyes off Sadie. She's worked her way under his skin."

"I think she's equally attracted. The sparks were flying." Joa pointed her glass at Keely and frowned. "And don't think that just because I'm engaging in this conversation, I'm not still mad at you. I am."

Keely didn't look remotely concerned. "You'll get over it. You always do. And, in time, you'll thank me."

When pigs flew.

Joa dropped her feet to the floor and leaned forward. The one thing she'd been certain of when she left New Zealand was that she didn't want to be an au pair again; she didn't want to be a part of someone else's family. Yes, she wanted a family of her own, but she needed to find it herself, make it herself. Or be alone. She was never again going to worm herself into someone else's life.

So acting as a nanny to Ronan's admittedly adorable sons wasn't something she wanted to do.

Keely looked at her with suddenly serious eyes. "Ronan needs help, Joa."

That wasn't her problem. "Are you seriously telling me he can't find one suitable nanny in a city this big?"

"He's tried, but he has the worst luck. They are either too old or too strict, or too young and too flirty. A bunch of them used his kids to insert themselves into his life, a couple going far enough to offer more than child-minding services."

Well, that was what happened when you were impossibly good-looking, rich and charming. Joa sighed, unable to tell Keely that she'd spent the past years pining after her two single bosses, over men she couldn't have, hiding her attraction from them because she hadn't wanted to make things awkward and embarrass herself. But if her attraction to them was a gentle, bubbling brook, then what she felt for Ronan was a raging, turbulent, fast-flowing river.

And she couldn't swim...

Then Joa made the mistake of meeting Keely's eyes and she saw the worry reflected in those brown depths. Knowing she wouldn't like what Keely was about to say, Joa held her breath.

"He's a very good friend, Ju, and he needs help. He's sad and stressed and he's barely keeping his head above water."

"Why me?" Joa wailed.

"Because you have the experience and the time. And you're the most levelheaded, down-to-earth person I know," Keely replied. "You're not impressed by his name, his looks—"

Oh, she was, but she'd rather die than admit that!

"—and you absolutely do not need his money. Help him out for a couple of months and maybe you can find a nanny for him...someone suitable. Besides, you know you will go off your head if you don't do something."

True. She hated being idle and, since Keely sometimes watched Ronan's boys, Joa had heard about Sam and Aron; apparently they were old enough to be interesting, young enough not to give Keely too much grief. And, yeah, maybe Ronan was at the end of his rope.

She wanted to help—she would help anyone if she could—but she just wished Ronan weren't quite so attractive.

Crap. Joa narrowed her eyes and pointed her index finger at her non-blood sister. "If I do this, and that's still a very remote possibility, you are so going to owe me, Keels."

Keely flashed her an impish grin. "Oh, I don't know. I think you might end up owing me."

And what, exactly, did she mean by *that*?

"Are you okay?"

Sadie put her hand on the door to the sushi bar and yanked it open. She and Beth had been trying to have dinner for weeks and they'd made plans earlier in the week to hit this sushi bar on Friday night. Sushi and sake, followed by, depending on how they felt, clubbing or bar hopping.

"I'm fine, why?" Sadie asked as they shed their coats.

"You're looking tired," Beth commented, draping her coat over her arm.

Sadie was feeling a little exhausted and, she decided, as she ran a finger between the band of her skirt and her shirt, a little bloated. She needed to drink more water and eat more vegetables and she would...

Tomorrow. After she'd gorged on sake and sushi.

"I'm fine. I've just been working hard," Sadie told her as she followed Beth across the restaurant to the corner seats. It was a great restaurant and as soon as she had a margarita in her hand, she'd be happy.

Beth placed an order for two margaritas—sake would come later—with the waitress before turning to Sadie

"Do you know that only the heart of the agave plant is used to make tequila?"

Sadie smiled. "I did not know that."

Beth pulled a face at Sadie's amused smile. "You know I collect useless facts," Beth said. "Do you know that earthworms have five hearts? I learned that today."

"I did not know that," Sadie repeated her previous sentence. She grinned, enjoying her friend's casual conversation. "Anything else you think I should know?"

Beth leaned back so the waitress could put their margaritas on the counter and Sadie was impressed by their ability to deliver their drinks that fast.

"I also know that *dibble* means to drink like a duck, butterflies taste with their feet and that you slept with Carrick Murphy."

How on earth did butterflies taste... *What?*

"Uh..." Sadie reached for her glass, shoved the straw into her mouth while she decided how to respond. Denying it would be a lie and she didn't like lying, especially to her friends. But she had slept with Beth's ex-brother-in-law.

And Beth was very obviously not happy with her.

"There's no point in denying it, Sadie Slade," Beth told her, blue eyes concerned. "Your eyes get all squinty when you lie and you always, always wiggle in your chair."

Sadie frowned at her and shifted in her seat. "I do not!"

"You so do," Beth said. "Are you really going to look me in the eye and tell me you didn't?"

Sadie looked glum. "No. And yes, we did."

Beth winced and her expression darkened. "When?"

Did it matter? "Nearly a month back. He came around to my apartment the day after I was taken to the hospital to check up on me."

"Sounds like he checked you out really, really well," Beth stated, sarcasm personified.

He did. Very well indeed. Numerous times, to be precise. But that wasn't something she could share with Beth because her friend was pissed. It was time to do damage control. Sadie lifted her hand, wanting to avoid a lecture. "It was one night, Beth. And nothing to get excited about."

Sadie really wished she could open up to Beth, tell her that she'd loved being with Carrick, that, for the first time in her life, she'd felt totally at ease in a man's arms. That, despite all the things she'd heard about him, Carrick made her feel both powerful and protected, treasured and cherished.

But Carrick was Beth's ex-brother-in-law and Tamlyn was sort of Sadie's friend. While Sadie didn't believe she'd done anything wrong by sleeping with him—they were both single, unattached adults—it still wasn't something she could freely discuss.

Not that she would talk intimacies, but Sadie thought the less said, the better this conversation would go.

"Carrick treated Tamlyn badly, Sadie. He was rude and ugly, ridiculously demanding and his behavior was destructive. His lawyers took her to the cleaners. He put down Jazz to spite her."

Jazz, Tamlyn's beloved golden Lab. Sadie still found it hard to square the Carrick she knew with a man who'd punish a dog to get revenge on his ex. She simply couldn't reconcile the two versions of the same man.

But...

But it didn't matter what Carrick did or didn't do

in the past; they'd shared their bodies and a slice of time. That was all. They now had a formal business relationship, nothing more. That suited her just fine.

"I'm not seeing him again, Beth," Sadie said. "I'm not getting involved with him. It was one night."

"And do you regret it?"

She knew Beth wanted her to say she did but she couldn't. She didn't regret a damn thing. Being with Carrick had been one of the best experiences of her life.

"Let's not talk about it anymore, Beth," Sadie said, feeling drained and a little emotional. Sadie blinked away burning tears, suddenly missing her apartment in Montparnasse. She missed her books, her brightly colored walls, her plants and her pillows. She missed the smell of croissants wafting up from the bakery below, the excitable French, the fresh food market down the road.

"Look, I know you are worried about me, but let's not get carried away, okay? I have seen and spoken to Carrick since that night and we are both behaving like nothing happened."

Seeing a new batch of sushi coming down the conveyor belt, Beth reached for an empty bowl and poured soy sauce into it. After stirring the sauce with her chopstick, her eyes met Sadie's. "So was it good?"

Good was such a weak word for how it had been between them. *Amazing* worked. *Unbelievable* was better. But Sadie couldn't share even the smallest detail with Beth. What happened between Sadie and

Carrick was theirs and sharing any part of it would dilute the memory of the evening.

She couldn't do it. She didn't have that many perfect evenings. She couldn't mess up the memory of the one completely perfect sexual encounter she did have.

Sadie sent her friend another hard stare, and Beth pursed her lips. "Okay, message received. We're done talking about Carrick."

Thank God. "Anything I should know about at work?" Sadie took another small sip of her margarita and wrinkled her nose. It didn't taste as good as it normally did.

Beth ran through a couple of potential projects, one of which was an appraisal for a Basquiat recently acquired by the Metropolitan Museum of Art. "Hey, did you hear about the lost Gauguin discovered in an attic in France?"

A neutral topic, yay. Sadie threw herself into the conversation, conscious that she and Beth were trying a little too hard to have fun.

Beth reached for a plate of nigiri and put it between them and Beth popped a piece into her mouth. She waved her chopstick at her plate. "Eat something."

Sadie lifted her margarita to her nose and sniffed. "Does this margarita taste right?"

Beth took Sadie's glass and a long sip of her drink and nodded enthusiastically. "It's perfect."

Huh. Weird. Either way, she didn't think she could drink it anymore. Maybe she was coming down with a tummy bug, or the flu.

Beth reached for a plate of sashimi and Sadie pulled back as the smell hit her nostrils. She was definitely getting sick. She had to be because this was one of the best sushi restaurants in the city and they maintained exceptionally high standards.

"What is wrong with you?" Beth demanded, placing her chopsticks across the rim of her sushi bowl. "You've turned this amazing shade of green."

Sadie looked down at the food and her stomach lurched. "It smells like fish."

"It *is* fish, Sadie. That's what sushi is…raw fish."

Sadie's stomach crawled up her throat and she placed her hand over her mouth. "I need to get out of here, Beth. Like now!"

"Oh, crap!" Beth hopped off the chair and scrambled in her bag for her wallet. Pulling out a couple of twenties, she placed them on the counter and took a moment to down the rest of her margarita.

"Not letting that go to waste," she muttered, handing Sadie her coat.

Sadie pulled her coat on and pulled it across her body. "Ugh, I don't feel well."

Beth nodded slowly. "I've heard there's a nasty tummy bug going around."

Marvelous.

Sadie let Beth lead her out of the restaurant, sending the waitress an apologetic glance. "But look on the bright side…?" Beth suggested as they stepped through the door into the frigid evening air.

Sadie was as nauseated as hell and felt as weak as

a day-old mouse. Was there a bright side? "And what might that be?"

"You could be telling me you're pregnant. Now, that would be a disaster of epic proportions. At least with a bug, it'll be over in a day or two."

Beth sighed when Sadie scowled. "I'm joking, Sadie. Look, I'll call you a cab. You should go home and climb into bed. Throw some Vitamin C down your throat and have an early night. I think I might carry on. I have friends at the Copper Kettle. I'm going to join them."

Sadie nodded, happy to be alone, as her world tilted slowly off its axis.

She didn't need an early night or to drink Vitamin C. What she really needed was a test. Because she had the gut-wrenching feeling that her so-called bug was going to be around for the rest of her life.

Four

Hi, I need to talk to you. Tonight. Can we meet?

Carrick's reply was almost instantaneous.

Okay. When? And where?

Now. I'm outside your front door.

Sadie tucked her phone away, thinking that she not only had a baby growing in her womb and a million butterflies buzzing, but she also had anxiety and fear gnawing holes in her stomach lining. And, worst of all, guilt kept washing over her, hot and sour. She should've been more careful about contraception, paid better attention. But as far as she could remember,

Carrick had worn a condom. What more could they have done?

But really, she couldn't shake the feeling that it was completely stupid to get pregnant in the twenty-first century. And deeply irresponsible. She was better than this, dammit, *smarter*.

But accidents, so they said, happened. This one was a multicar pileup.

Sadie had spent the past week thinking about her options, deciding what to do. She'd sent Carrick a message earlier in the week telling him she was going out of town to do an appraisal in New York, but she'd lied; she'd just holed up in her apartment and paced the floor.

There was a baby growing in her womb—a combination of her and Carrick—and she'd spent a lot of time deciding how to proceed. It wasn't the eighteen hundreds, and she had options, but Sadie knew she'd have to live with any, and all, of her choices.

She was staunchly pro-choice, firmly believing it was a woman's right to make decisions about her own body. But up until this moment, pro-choice had always been an intellectual concept, something she believed in, but didn't expect to face.

After days of rigorous internal debate, she'd made the decision to keep the baby. When she married, she'd wanted to get pregnant straightaway, but it hadn't happened. After her divorce she'd been grateful to be spared the ordeal of raising a child with Dennis. He hated having to share her attention and it wouldn't have mattered that it was his child taking her attention away.

Dennis was all about Dennis…

Ironic that she was pregnant by a guy who was reputedly so much like her ex-husband. She wished she was nice enough, a good enough person, not to fret about how much of Carrick's personality her baby would inherit—and damn, she'd nurture the hell out of this baby to make sure he or she didn't grow up to be a jerk—but she had worried. Worried still.

But at the end of the day, giving the baby up for adoption or having an abortion was out of the question because she'd always planned on having a child, maybe two, in the future, with or without a man. She could afford to raise a child; money wasn't a problem. She'd have to cut back on her traveling but that was a bridge she'd cross when she had to. Having a child was part of her life plan; the timing was just earlier than she'd expected.

Sadie was already excited about having a person in her life she could unconditionally love. She already loved him, or her, loved the little bundle of cells growing inside her. Being a mother didn't scare her, but telling Carrick she was pregnant with his child did.

How would she tell him? How would he react? What would he say after she broke the news?

Sadie shuffled from foot to foot, wondering why he was taking so long to open his front door. She turned around and looked out into the misty night, tendrils of dense fog touching her cheeks and forehead. It was the end of January; the baby would be born in late September, early October.

So near, yet so far away.

Sadie heard the snick of a lock and resisted the urge to bolt down the path and fling herself into her leased car. In an hour she could be at the airport; in another few hours she could be on a plane heading for Paris, or she could go to the UAE and hide out at Hassan's apartment in Abu Dhabi. He wouldn't ask any questions; in fact, he'd offer her marriage to keep her in the lap of luxury. There were benefits to having an Arabian prince as a best friend.

But his family, as much as they adored her, would not approve of their son raising another man's child. She didn't need Hassan's parental help, nor did she need his financial help.

She just needed to not have this conversation with Carrick Murphy.

"Sorry, I'd just stepped out of the shower when you sent that message. That's why I took so long," Carrick said after opening the imposing front door to his house. He stepped back into the hallway and gestured her inside.

Sadie stepped into his hall, her eyes immediately going to the massive abstract painting on the large wall on her right. She unwound her scarf as she hustled over to the painting, wanting to fall into all that movement and color. Carrick was so lucky to see this painting every single day.

"When did you acquire this Pollack?" Sadie demanded. "I don't know this painting."

"My grandfather bought it in the forties from the artist himself." Carrick tugged her coat from her shoulders and Sadie barely noticed.

"What's it called?"

"Sadie, you didn't come to my house at ten at night to discuss art," Carrick said, hanging her coat and scarf on an antique coat stand in the corner. He frowned at her. "Or did you? Is this about the Homer?"

She wished. Sadie shook her head and pushed her hands into the back pockets of her jeans. "Can we… can we sit?"

Carrick nodded. "Okay. Let's go to the library."

Sadie followed him down the hallway, admiring his gorgeous butt in soft, faded jeans and the width of his shoulders covered by a thin, loose, long-sleeved shirt. His big, broad feet were bare on the harlequin-checked floor. Sadie's eyes kept darting from his ass to the walls, equally fascinated by the art she kept passing. Was that a Picasso? A pencil sketch by Lucien Freud? A Rothko?

Carrick hung back to allow her to enter the library first and Sadie sucked in her breath at the floor-to-ceiling shelves and the massive desk holding a laptop and a printer. On the opposite side of the room, the shelves had been removed and a large fireplace dominated the space, in front of which stood two club chairs and a long, slightly worn leather sofa. The room was warm and cozy and all she wanted to do was to lie on the couch and fall asleep.

Carrick went over to the drinks cabinet in the corner and lifted a crystal decanter. "Do you want a drink?"

Sadie shook her head and perched on the end of one of the club chairs. She placed her hands between her knees. "No, thank you."

"Coffee? Tea?" Carrick asked, pouring some whiskey into a glass.

"No, I'm fine. I don't need anything but for you to come and sit down so I can talk to you."

Carrick frowned at her, but he walked over to the sofa and sat down, propping his bare feet up on the coffee table. He took a sip of his whiskey, swallowed and handed her an easy smile. "Why so serious, Sadie? Are you going to tell me you are pregnant?"

He said it lightly, like there was no possibility of that happening. She was about to burst that bubble and burst it hard. "Yeah. That's exactly why I'm here."

Carrick's hand around his glass tightened and his eyes sharpened, but that was all the reaction she received. "That's not even vaguely funny, Sadie."

She wasn't laughing. "I doubt this is something you wanted to hear, but I *am* pregnant and since you're the only person I've slept with since my divorce, you're the father. I thought I owed it to you to tell you that I'm carrying your child."

"What?"

Sadie didn't give him time to catch up. "Look, I know this is a shock and that you need time to let this sink in. When it does, the only thing you need to decide is what kind of dad you would like to be. It's up to you if you want to support your child and be part of this journey, part of your child's life."

There. It was out now. She just had to wait for his

reaction. Would it be explosive, vitriolic? Would he throw something, scream at her, blame her? Would she finally see the guy Tamlyn had lived with?

Show me your true colors, Murphy. Let's get it over with.

She waited a minute, then another. Carrick just stared at her, his expression begging her to take back her words. Unfortunately, a do-over wasn't possible.

Thinking that they both needed some time to process this life-changing news, Sadie stood up. "Let me know what you decide. I'll see myself out."

Carrick felt the burn of whiskey as it slid down his throat, thinking that he couldn't possibly have interpreted Sadie's words correctly. It wasn't possible. She couldn't be pregnant. He'd used condoms that night, he was sure of it.

Using condoms was as much second nature to him as brushing his teeth. Or shaving. He rubbed his jaw and felt his two-day stubble. Okay, maybe shaving wasn't a good analogy since that was something he occasionally neglected.

He never, ever neglected his teeth. Or failed to protect himself or his partner.

"How?" he asked, hearing the croak in his voice.

Sadie sank back down to the chair and lifted her shoulders. At least she wasn't pretending to misunderstand him. "The condom could've slipped or fallen off or torn. It might've been faulty."

Surely he would've noticed a broken condom? Then again, he'd been so caught up in the smell and taste and wonder of Sadie that a nuclear bomb could've dropped next door and he might not have noticed.

Honestly? The chances of him noticing a split or leaking condom hovered around zero.

Carrick racked his brain and tried to recall any housekeeping he'd done that night he'd loved her so thoroughly and drew a blank. Sadie's soft skin, her smell, her moans... Those he remembered in Technicolor. Getting rid of condoms? Not so much.

He opened his mouth to speak and immediately snapped it closed again. What was there to say? Sorry? He could express regret, but would it change a damn thing? No, it wouldn't.

And was he *really* sorry?

He was surprised, shocked. His world had been kicked off its axis, but was he sorry? He wasn't sure that he was.

He'd always wanted a kid and when he said goodbye to his marriage, he'd said goodbye to that dream, too. He believed kids should be raised within a committed relationship and since he'd had no intention of jumping into that alligator-infested swamp again, he resigned himself to a child-free life.

But Sadie was pregnant, the kid was his and he had another shot at being a father, something he'd believed was beyond his grasp.

He wasn't delighted, but he wasn't about to chew his wrists off, either.

Sadie had asked what role he wanted to play in his child's life—he could see from her expression she was expecting him to bail—but there was one thing he was sure of...

He fully intended to be this child's father, in every way that counted. From child support to midnight feedings, to changing diapers and bath time and bedtime reading, he intended to be there every step of the way. How they were going to make that work when they were living in two separate houses, in two separate countries, was something they still had to discuss.

But he'd figure it out; he had nine months—eight?—before that became an issue.

He had plenty of time.

Sadie scooted to the edge of her seat, looking like she'd rather be anywhere but here. "Look, you obviously need time for this to sink in so I think I should go."

Carrick stood up and walked back to the array of drinks across the room. He poured another whiskey and wished he could offer her one since she looked dead on her feet. Judging by her raccoon eyes, it was obvious that she'd had minimal sleep this past week. She looked pale and played out and she wasn't going anywhere.

Not just yet.

"Stay, Sadie, we have things to discuss."

"Except that you aren't saying anything," Sadie pointed out as she stood up. "I'm trying to give you some time to make sense of this craziness, Carrick."

Carrick saw her sway on her feet and he bounded over to her and placed his hands on her shoulders, pushing her down onto the comfortable cushions. Ignoring her protests, he pulled off her flat-soled boots

and dropped them onto the carpet. Yanking a cashmere blanket from the arm of the leather sofa, he
draped it over her knees and looked at the fireplace.
"I can make a fire if you are cold."

Sadie flung the blanket off her knees, her expression mutinous. "Carrick! I'm fine, for crying out loud."

He didn't believe her since she looked a degree
warmer than a corpse. "Will you just wait there, for
five minutes or so?"

"Where are you going?"

Pregnancy hadn't robbed her of her sassy personality. Good to know. "I'm just going to make you a
cup of hot chocolate. I figure if you can't have alco-
hol, then chocolate is the next best thing."

Sadie released a huff and he saw the frustration in
those hundred shades of blue. "Carrick, I don't need
a fire, or a blanket or hot chocolate. I need you to sit
down and talk to me about the baby I'm carrying."

Carrick dug his toes into the antique Persian beneath his feet. "I need five minutes, Sadie, alone. I
also need to do something, so I'm going to make you
hot chocolate. You might not want it, but I need to
make it because I need a little space. When I get back,
I'll try and form a rational response."

Carrick headed for the door and her soft question
nearly dropped him to his knees. "Are you mad? At
me?"

He turned to see her looking down at her hands,
her shoulders shaking. He fought the urge to rush to
her side, to pull her into his arms and tell her that ev-

erything would be fine. But he couldn't because who knew what else life had in store for them?

But it was important that she understand what he was about to say next. He walked back to her, dropped to his haunches in front of her and placed his hands on her knees.

"Sadie, I'm not blaming you. I'm not even blaming myself because it would be futile. We are adults. We took precautions. Sure, everyone says that condoms are effective, but we are proof they are not. The only foolproof method of birth control is abstinence and abstinence sucks. So no, I'm not mad at you. Surprised, shocked, weirded out, sure, but mad? No."

Carrick held her gaze and watched as tension seeped from her as air would exit a leaky balloon. Her shoulders dropped below her ears, her fists uncurled and her lips softened. She looked relieved, but still completely wiped out.

He would bet the artwork in this house that if she curled up in that chair, if she tucked a pillow behind her head, she would be asleep in ten minutes, maybe less. The thing was, he didn't want her to fall asleep. He wanted her naked and writhing, moaning his name as he slid inside her.

She'd just handed him news big enough to tilt his world off his axis and all he wanted to do was make love to her? Carrick scrubbed his face with his hands.

What the hell, dude?

"I'll be back in a few. Relax," Carrick told her as he stood up, wincing at the inanity. "Try to relax,"

he corrected himself, before tapping the door frame
and heading for the kitchen.

He knew that in the cupboard above the fridge was
an unopened bottle of Jack and he intended to crack
that bottle open and take a belt or four.

It was that type of night.

Sadie woke up lying on Carrick, chest to chest,
her stomach dented by a very long, very hard, erection, her face in his neck. His hand was between her
loose jeans and her panties, holding most of her right
butt cheek, and his other hand was under her shirt,
his fingers under her bra strap between her shoulder
blades. Murphy had, sometime during the night, been
desperate to find some skin.

And really, since his touch felt like sunshine, Sadie
had no objections.

Sadie yawned as she remembered him going to the
kitchen, something about him making hot chocolate
she didn't want. She had a vague recollection of snug-
gling down into that enormously comfortable chair,
then the memory of strong arms lifting her up to rest
against his wide chest.

He'd lowered her to the sofa and followed her
down and she'd thought that she should object. Instead of pulling away, she'd simply curled into him;
his warmth was temptation personified and his smell
addictive.

And she'd dropped into sleep.

Last night she'd been too tired to pull away, to put
some distance between them, but in the cold light of

morning, she knew that being nose to nose, groin to groin, plastered against Carrick Murphy was not a smart idea. Before she did anything stupid—like kiss him—she needed to disentangle herself, preferably with grace and ease.

Or simply disentangle herself.

Carrick, as if sensing she was ready to bolt, pulled her closer. "You feel so amazing, so soft. And, God, your smell."

Sadie tensed, wondering what he meant. Okay, time to get up and sort herself out. Sadie moved her hands to push against him, but his hand on her butt pushed her into his erection, and his hand on her back mashed her breasts against his chest. "Where are you going?" Carrick mumbled.

"Getting off you." Surely her actions were self-explanatory?

"Why?"

Because if I don't, I might just start ripping off your clothes.

And that would add gas to the already smoldering dumpster fire they were currently feeding.

"Not ready to get up and certainly not ready to face the day."

Sadie pulled her head back to look at Carrick. His eyelashes brushed his skin, surprisingly long. His beard was thicker than she'd ever seen it and she wanted to run her fingers through his stubble while she kissed those sexy lips.

"We need to get to work, Murphy," Sadie whispered, a small part of her—okay, all of her—hoping he would disagree with her and either urge her to go back to sleep or, even better, to get naked.

Bad Sadie.

"I just want to lie here and touch you, Sadie." Carrick opened one eye and lifted his wrist to squint at his watch. "It's barely even six, far too early to consider moving."

"Then I should go, let you get some decent sleep."

"What makes you think I didn't sleep?" Carrick asked, his fingers drawing patterns on the skin of her butt.

She'd spent the night lying on top of him; he couldn't have been comfortable.

"You weigh next to nothing and I love having you in my arms." He lifted his hips and pushed his erection into her. "Can't you tell?"

"I'd be impressed if it wasn't something all men wake up with daily," Sadie replied, telling herself not to shift her hips to maximize her pleasure. "And may I point out that's what got us into trouble in the first place?"

Despite how amazing she felt, and how tempted she was, she couldn't forget that there was only one reason why she was here. Through their growing baby, she was now tethered to this man for the next eighteen to forever years.

"Best night of my life," Carrick murmured, dropping a kiss into her hair. Carrick shifted her so his shaft was aligned with her mound and Sadie released a low groan. She couldn't help it; he felt so damn good. She pressed down, closed her eyes and allowed pleasure to slide through her.

Her desire was tinged with relief, with a lot of "thank God, that went better than I thought." She'd expected fireworks last night, smashed glasses, a whole bunch of yelling, but Carrick's response to becoming a father had been measured, even—dare she say it?—thoughtful.

She wasn't about to completely reverse her opinion that he was a bad boy, but maybe he wasn't quite as bad as she'd painted him to be. And while it didn't mean anything, couldn't mean anything, she felt so damn good lying in his arms.

Then she made the mistake of opening her eyes, lifting them to look at Carrick. Light green clashed with blue and they stared at each other for a moment and later, Sadie couldn't remember who made the first move. Was it him, was it her? Either way, their mouths connected in a flurry of teeth and lips and tongue. He tasted like sex and sleep, a heady combination that melted her thought processes. All she knew for sure was that she wanted to get naked as soon as possible.

At least she couldn't get pregnant this time. The thought hit her with all the power of a missile strike. She was pregnant. They hadn't discussed the future, she was having a baby with this man and they had a million decisions to make.

Sex should be way down on their priority list.

She should be sensible, responsible. This was complete craziness.

"Carrick…" Sadie whispered his name against his lips, trying to ignore his hand kneading her butt.

"Mmm?"

"Is this a good idea?"

"Probably not," Carrick admitted, his voice rough with need. "But let's do it anyway. In an hour or two we can return to real life, to reality, but for now, let's have this."

Sadie hesitated and Carrick cupped her face in his hands, his thumbs stroking her cheekbones. "Let's take this time, and just be. Let's enjoy each other and what we do to and for each other. The future can wait. Let's take this time before the day starts, before the rest of our lives change irrevocably and we drive each other crazy. It's just you and me, nobody else, nothing else matters."

How could she resist his low-pitched, rumbly voice, his sexy words? What woman in the world could? She thought she should remind him that this wasn't going to become a habit, that sleeping together this morning would be another onetime thing, but talking was for later…

Right now all she wanted to do was feel.

Sadie lowered her mouth to his, and Carrick's hand moved from her face to the back of her head, keeping her at the angle he preferred. His tongue swept inside her mouth. She felt him shudder, his erection hardening against her stomach. The first rays of dawn lightened the room and shadows danced across his skin as the day unfurled. Carrick made her feel like that, like she was new and precious and exciting, full of possibilities.

Sadie sat up and peeled herself off Carrick, sliding off him to look down at him. She kneeled next to the sofa and ran her hand over his chest, down the shaft tenting his pants. Carrick shuddered and his eyes took on a sheen of gold, his low murmurs of approval telling her how much he enjoyed her touch. The previous time they'd made love, Carrick had been in the driver's seat and this time, this last time, she wanted control.

Sadie pushed her hands up and under Carrick's shirt and pulled it up his chest, revealing a light dusting of hair, his ripped stomach and his muscled arms. Carrick pulled the shirt up and over his head, and Sadie placed her lips on his biceps, needing to feel the play of those big muscles under her lips. She inhaled his musky, soap-and-man-and-sex smell and felt that rush of warmth hitting her panties.

Yeah, she wanted him…so much it actually hurt.

"Come up here and kiss me," Carrick told her, looking at her through half-closed eyelids. He pushed his fingers into her hair, playing with her curls.

"Not yet," Sadie softly replied, placing her hand on his chest and feeling his heartbeat under her hand. So strong, so steady, so intensely male. She watched, fascinated, as his small nipple contracted and she impulsively put her mouth to that bud and was surprised at the low groan her touch elicited. Emboldened, she moved her mouth across his chest, touching her tongue to his warm skin. On her knees now, she caressed his sides and ran the back of her knuckles over his stomach before dipping her tongue into his sunken belly button.

"You're killing me here, Sades."

But in a good way. Sadie smiled against his skin and traced the ripples of his washboard stomach with her tongue.

"I need to touch you, Sadie."

"Not done, Murphy." Sadie placed her hand on his erection, sliding her fingers up his shaft, feeling the heat beneath the soft fabric of his jeans. She flipped open the buttons on his fly. Carrick placed his thumbs in the band of his jeans and lifted his hips, pushing them down. When they landed in a heap on the floor next to her knees, she stared down at him, entranced by his masculine beauty. She traced the raised veins with one finger, before spreading the small bead of moisture over its head.

She was soaking wet from just looking at him. She could slide her leg over him and he'd be inside her with no trouble at all, but if this was their last time—and it had to be—then she wanted to live out a little fantasy...

Or, judging by the size, a big fantasy.

She'd never done this before; she'd never wanted to with Dennis—and what did that say about her marriage?—but how hard could it be? Sadie placed her lips on his shaft and inhaled his sexy scent. Placing her lips on him, she nibbled her way up to his head before resting the tip on her closed mouth.

"Dying here, Sadie. Seriously," Carrick muttered, lifting his hips to encourage her to open her mouth.

Sadie turned her head to look at him, pulling her

hair back behind her ear to see him clearly. "Do you want me to continue, Carrick?"

"More than I want my heart to keep beating," he replied, his voice vibrating with need.

She liked the note of desperation she heard in his voice, the way his erratic breathing filled the room. For once the mighty Murphy wasn't in control—she was, and she felt powerful, feminine, alluring. Sexy, dammit.

And in giving, she was ramping up her own pleasure; she'd never been more turned on in her life. Sadie opened her mouth and allowed his erection to slide onto her tongue, her lips closing around him. She felt Carrick tense, and his hand in her hair tightened.

"Feels so good, Sadie. God, please don't stop."

Sadie took him deeper and she swirled her tongue around his tip and Carrick released a low stream of curses. Using his core muscles to sit up, he gently pulled her head back. "Too much," he muttered.

"Can't handle me, Murphy?" Sadie teased him.

"Damn straight. Not when you do that." Carrick's words were rough with suppressed need and emotion. He swung his feet off the couch, pulled her to stand between his knees and quickly divested her of her clothing. When she was naked in front of him, he placed his forehead between her breasts and gripped her waist with his hands. "Want you so much, Sadie."

She was here, she was naked, why was he waiting? Sadie felt him kiss her skin, his hands moving up to cover her breasts, his thumbs brushing over her nipples in a light but make-me-crazy touch. "I need you inside me, Carrick, filling me, stretching me, making me whole."

"Give me a sec, honey, I'm so close."

She didn't want him in control; she wanted him wild and unhinged and thoughtless. Taking the initiative again, she pushed him back down and Sadie straddled him, brushing her wet warmth against his erection. Pleasure slid through her, warm and wet and wonderful. Not giving Carrick much time to react, she took him in hand, lifted her hips and slid down onto him, sighing as he filled her.

They'd only been together once before, but she'd missed this. Missed him.

Carrick pulled her close so that her breasts pushed into his chest, his arm snaking up her back to hold her head. He kissed her fiercely, and Sadie wasn't sure where he started and she left off. For the first time in her life—okay, technically the second time—she felt completely immersed in someone else, like his heart was beating for her, like she breathed for him.

It was powerful, insanely powerful, and Sadie felt her stomach and heart contract. With pleasure, in awe and with a healthy dose of fear that she might never feel this way again.

"Sadie, honey, I need you to come because I can't hold on," Carrick muttered, his hips lifting, sliding in deeper. He repeated the motion and Sadie's eyes crossed as she chased that tornado of pleasure across the dawn sky. Carrick pushed his hand between them and found her bud, rolling it under his finger. She hurtled toward the maelstrom, flying faster and faster until she was close enough to step into it and then she was falling, tumbling, screaming, riding, hurtling...

Bands of pleasure tossed her around and then Carrick pistoned into her and she felt his release deep inside. She wrapped her arms around his neck and held her face against his, not wanting to step off this awesome ride.

Her twister of pleasure slowly dissipated and Sadie released her tight grip on Carrick, her muscles loosening as she sank against him, confident he'd hold her weight. She felt breathless, weightless and crazy satisfied.

Carrick's hand drifted over her head, down her back. He was still inside her and she had no intention of moving, not just yet.

"What the hell was that?" he softly asked.

Sadie dropped a kiss on his collarbone before placing her hands on his chest and pushing herself up. "Good sex?"

"Great sex," Carrick corrected her. She felt him harden inside her and was astounded by the wave of pleasure that shot up her spine.

She'd genuinely thought she was done. Her last orgasm had been so intense, she didn't think she was up for a repeat... Not so soon anyway.

Then Carrick smiled, dropped his hand to where their bodies joined and found her wet and wanting and throbbing.

"I thought we were done," she softly said, looking at his sexy mouth.

"Hell, no, we're just getting started."

Five

After taking a shower in Carrick's enormous en-suite bathroom, Sadie pulled on her clothes and walked back into his bedroom. It was dominated by an enormous king-size bed and an oversize oil painting above the headboard. Ignoring Carrick, who sat on the edge of the bed, dressed and pulling on a pair of socks, she crawled across the mattress to kneel on the pillows, searching for a signature on the painting. It was an impressionist landscape in greens and blues, a French river at dawn.

Was it a Monet, a Manet? Judging by the breath-taking art elsewhere in the house, she wouldn't be surprised.

"You're wasting your time. There is no signature," Carrick told her, amusement in his voice.

Sadie frowned at the painting. That wasn't possible; he must have missed it. This painting was too good not to be documented. "Who is it by?"

Carrick shrugged. "We have no idea. We have no record of how it came into the family, who the artist is, absolutely nothing."

That simply wasn't possible. A painting of this quality had to have left its mark; there had to be a record of it somewhere. Sadie touched the side of the frame with reverent fingers as if it could speak to her.

"Have you researched it?"

"To death," Carrick replied, standing up to tuck his button-down shirt into his pants. "I've researched it, Finn has researched it, my folks did the same. There's nothing to be found."

Sadie refused to accept that. "I could try."

Carrick grinned. "Go for it, but I'm not paying you another exorbitant fee for you to trace down leads I know aren't there."

"I'll do it pro bono." Sadie sat back on her heels and stared at the landscape, falling into the picture. There was something incredibly familiar about the painting, as if she recognized the artist or the subject or the brushstrokes. She'd spent time with this artist or scene before...she just needed to recall who and when and where.

Carrick's arm around her waist wrenched her back to the present. He pulled her up against his chest, but when her feet touched the floor, he didn't release her.

"How are you feeling?" he asked, his breath warm against the shell of her ear.

Since she'd started the morning with multiple orgasms, she felt absolutely fantastic. "Awesome. All loosey-goosey."

Sadie felt the rumble of his laughter. "Good to know, but I was actually referring to this." He tapped her flat stomach with his index finger.

Oh. Oh, right. She was pregnant with his child. Between the fabulous sex and the jaw-dropping art, she'd forgotten she was going to be a mommy. Her breath hitched and her heart threatened to jump out of her chest. "Fine."

"No nausea, tiredness, food cravings?"

Sadie stepped back and Carrick's arms fell to his sides. "How do you know about pregnancy symptoms?"

Carrick's shoulder lifted and fell. "Ronan has two boys, and he gave us a blow by blow of Thandi's pregnancies."

She hadn't known Ronan was married and told Carrick so.

Grief flashed in Carrick's eyes. "She died shortly after the birth of Aron, their second son. She started hemorrhaging and they couldn't stop it in time."

Sadie winced. "That's horrible. I'm so sorry."

"It was a rough time," Carrick admitted. "We all adored Thandi, and Ronan still grieves for his wife."

"I think he probably always will," Sadie softly replied.

Carrick ran his hand through his damp hair. "So back to you. How are you feeling?" His lips quirked upward. "With reference to your pregnancy, not the sex."

Sadie returned his smile. "I really am fine. I haven't had any nausea and I'm as energetic as ever. I'm not very far along so everything is mostly as it was."

"I'd believe that if you hadn't fallen asleep in the chair last night without waking up when I moved you to the sofa," Carrick pointed out.

Sadie crossed her arms and rocked on her heels. "I haven't slept much this past week. I've been making plans. And rehearsing the best way to tell you."

Carrick frowned at her. "I'm that unapproachable?"

Sadie sat down on the edge of the bed and rested her forearms on her knees. "I don't expect it's ever easy telling a guy you're pregnant. And honestly, I didn't expect you to react as calmly as you did."

Carrick walked into his closet and returned with a cobalt-blue tie, which he draped around his neck. He started to knot the ends, his eyes on hers. "I don't believe in beating the horse because I left the stable door open. What's done is done. We must deal with what is, not how we wish it to be."

"Talking of dealing with what is—" Sadie linked her fingers between her knees "—how are we going to do this, moving forward?"

Carrick looked at her and Sadie felt pinned to the floor. "What exactly are you asking me, Sadie?"

Sadie had to smile at the panic flashing in his eyes. "I'm not asking you to marry me, Carrick. I'm just looking for an indication of whether you'd like to be a part of the baby's life. Or whether you intend to bail."

"First, I've never bailed on a thing in my life."

Carrick had bailed on his marriage, but then again, so had she. Sometimes it was okay to walk away from toxic people and situations. Unfortunately, according to Tamlyn and Beth, Carrick had been the source of that toxicity.

But since Sadie was neither marrying him nor falling in love with him, and as long as he kept any toxic behavior away from her baby, that wasn't something she needed to worry about.

"And, gut reaction, I want the baby. I might not want a relationship—" yeah, she heard his warning, thank you very much "—but I do want to be a dad."

Well, then. Okay.

"But we don't need to decide on the mechanics of our relationship today. We have time. Have you told anyone else you are pregnant?"

"No, why?"

"When the news breaks, the tabloids will make a big deal about it." Carrick's mouth turned down and his face hardened. "The press will devour this news. It will be a big deal. First pregnancies, so I'm told, often end in miscarriage so I'd prefer only to weather one storm of press attention. I'd hate to have to go back and explain that you've miscarried."

"Would the press really be that interested in this?"

"Oh, hell, yes," Carrick muttered, and Sadie recalled the internet search she'd done on him and the many articles she'd found detailing the most sordid aspects of his marriage.

The press loved drama, especially within a high profile family like the Murphys, and there had been a lot of it five years ago.

Carrick's suggestion to wait made sense so Sadie nodded. "I'm happy to keep it a secret. It's nobody's business but our own."

"Talking about miscarriages, are you expecting any problems?" Carrick asked. "Do you have a family history of miscarriages? God, do you even have a family?"

Sadie had to laugh. "I wasn't found under a banana tree, Murphy."

Carrick pulled a face. "For someone I'm having a baby with, I know next to nothing about you."

That was true. They'd shared their bodies, the most intimate of physical acts, but they knew next to nothing about each other. "I'm the third of four kids and as far as I know, my mom popped us out with no trouble at all."

Carrick rubbed his jaw. "I think we need to change that, Sadie."

Change what?

"If we are going to raise a child together, the least we can be is friends," Carrick said, choosing his words with care. "We have this hectic attraction, but that's not going to help us raise a child together. We need to get to know each other."

Sadie stared at him, suddenly realizing that she wasn't in this alone; she was going to have a father for her child. Despite knowing that she could, and would, raise a child by herself, she was so damn grateful that she didn't have to.

But their chemistry complicated the situation.

Sadie waved at the bed. "What about this?"

"Sex?"

Sadie placed her hand on the bed to anchor herself. She nodded, the edges of her vision a little fuzzy. "Uh-huh."

"Sex is sex, work is work, but there's no rule that says we can't be friends and not have sex, that we can't work together and not have sex."

He was being so very rational, so damn reasonable. She'd expected a completely different reaction—a lot more fire and brimstone—and she was so grateful to have avoided a nasty scene. Sadie bit her lip, fighting tears. It had all gone so much better than she'd expected. Emotion and exhaustion clashed and she felt herself drifting…

"You okay?" Carrick asked her, but his voice sounded like it was coming from a long way away.

Sadie felt her head rocking and the room darkened. Then the air disappeared and the carpet came up to smack her in the face.

"You fainted?"

Sadie heard the trace of amusement in Hassan's question and frowned at his image on the screen of her laptop. Hassan, in Abu Dhabi, leaned back in his office chair, looking elegant in a three-piece suit.

Yep, those deep brown eyes were definitely laughing at her. Sadie rubbed her forehead with the tips of her fingers. "I face-planted straight into the carpet. When I came around, Carrick gave me a lecture about my health and bundled me off to see a doctor."

"And what did the doctor say?"

Sadie sipped her peppermint tea before answering. She had work to do, but she needed to talk to her old friend. Technically, he was Prince Hassan Ramid El-Aboud, but she'd known Hassan since they were both new students at Princeton a decade ago. He'd studied engineering and she art history, and while she knew he was from Abu Dhabi, she hadn't known that he was a royal…

Royal as in the nephew of the reigning king of the United Arab Emirates.

Hassan might look like the Arab prince-hero of a romance novel, but to her, he was just her best friend. The person with whom she could share her and Carrick's secret. In her defense, Hassan was her closest friend and she knew Hassan was a vault.

"He said that I'm pregnant. That fainting is fairly common in pregnancy and that I'm as healthy as a horse. Carrick didn't believe him."

"How do you know?" Hassan asked.

"Because as we left the doctor's rooms, Carrick called his PA and told her to get me another appointment with another obstetrician." Sadie rolled her eyes. "He wants a second opinion."

Hassan laughed. "And are you going for a second opinion?"

"Don't be ridiculous. I'm pregnant, not ill," Sadie said, allowing her frustration to seep through.

Hassan tipped his head to the side. "And are you going to sleep with him again?"

Oh, she wished she could say no, but she knew that the chances of her and Carrick ending up in bed together again were astronomically high. "I want to tell you we won't, but I'd probably be lying."

Concern flashed in Hassan's eyes. "Sleeping with him is one thing, Sadie, but falling in love with him is another."

Sadie balanced her tea on her knee. "Who said anything about love?" she demanded.

Hassan's brown eyes reflected his concern. "How does Beth feel about you having Carrick's baby?"

Sadie grimaced. "I haven't told her."

Hassan's eyebrows rose. "You do know you can't keep it a secret from her forever?"

"Carrick asked me to keep my pregnancy between us until the first trimester has passed. I've told you, but I don't feel comfortable telling Beth, partly because Beth will lecture me about him, saying that he's not the type of man I need in my life, that he leaves destruction in his wake."

"She'd also say you already went through hell with Dennis. Why would you want to put yourself through that with Carrick?"

Strangely, Sadie's first instinct was to defend Carrick. She wanted to tell Hassan that Carrick was nothing like Dennis, but logic and practicality refused to allow her to do that. She wanted to believe Carrick wasn't anything like her ex, but she'd hardly spent any time with him.

And, let's be honest here, the time they'd spent together hadn't required talking.

Hassan leaned forward. "Look, I have no doubt that Tamlyn exaggerated Carrick's sins. She's not the type to take rejection lying down. But when you told me you were pregnant with his kid, I went online, did some research. I saw numerous photos of Carrick and his ex together. Sadie, they didn't look happy. He wasn't good for her."

But there was a difference between not being good for her and not being good *to* her. But no matter what had happened in his previous marriage, Carrick was going to be in Sadie's life for a long, long time. He was her child's father and they'd always have a bond.

But that didn't mean she had to be emotionally tied to him. They could be friends, be mutually respectful, but they didn't have to love each other to be effective coparents.

But it would be helpful if they could, at the very least, like each other, as she informed Hassan.

"I respect that, Sadie, I do, but I'm worried about you."

"What do you mean?"

Hassan looked frustrated. "You're an independent, strong woman, but a part of you still believes in the sanctity of a family unit, in bringing your child up with a mom and a dad, preferably in the same house. However you work this deal with Carrick, he's going to be a very big part of your life. Are you going to meet and date and fall in love with anyone else or are you going to fall for him because he's there and because he sets your panties on fire?"

It was a good question and one she didn't have an answer for. Sadie thought about her response. "When the baby comes, I'm not going to have time to date someone else, even if I wanted to. What's wrong with sleeping with Carrick as we coraise our child?"

"Because you are not the type who can separate sex from love on a long-term basis. If you don't learn to do that, you will fall for him, Sadie. And he might end up breaking your heart."

She was too smart to repeat past mistakes.

"He's not going to make me cry, Hassan."

"How can you be so sure, Sadie?"

"Because I won't let him," Sadie told Hassan, conviction in her voice. "There's too much at stake for me to be stupid and allow the guy to hurt me. I've got this, I promise."

"Oh, Sades, I wish I could believe you."

Ronan asked Joa for a meeting to discuss his lack-of-nanny situation and, as per his instructions, Joa walked down the icy path running along the side of Ronan's house and gingerly climbed the steps leading up to the pretty entertainment area off the kitchen. The steps were like oiled glass and her feet felt disconnected from her body.

She hadn't been back in Boston long and she was already over the snow, the cold and the wet. Her uniform for the past few years had been shorts, T-shirts and flip-flops, and she found dressing in layers an absolute pain.

Northern hemisphere winters were a huge con on her "should I permanently move back to Boston?" list.

Joa stepped into the sunroom—funny!—off the kitchen and started to disrobe: coat, hat, gloves and scarf. Feeling ten pounds lighter and dressed in a long-sleeved T-shirt and skinny jeans, she felt almost normal.

But damn, she did miss her flip-flops.

Joa walked into the kitchen, surprised by the quiet. In her experience, mornings in a household of kids was a madhouse and she'd expected the boys to be sitting down to breakfast with Ronan making their lunches or packing their bags. If he was anything like her other dads, then she'd expected to see him rushing around in an untucked button-down shirt, the ends of his tie on his chest, tailored suit pants and socks, talking to his kids, looking fine and yes, smelling gorgeous.

Joa tipped her head up to look at the ceiling, annoyed with herself. She thought she was done with behaving that way. None of her other dads could hold a candle looks wise to Ronan, but they were all good fathers.

And maybe that was the root of her fantasies, why she found herself so attracted to them: they were all about family.

Men who made being a good parent a priority was a huge turn-on for her and that was, surely, because she never had a father, or parents, of her own. Her mother had been useless and God only knew who her dad was.

But her crush on her previous employers had been more cerebral than physical, and her fantasies had revolved around what they represented: a family, having someone in her corner, a man who provided a constant source of love and security.

Safety.

Ronan wasn't safe at all.

He was a stressed-out, terse, snappy man and...

And she was physically attracted to him. Brutally, horribly so.

And she'd rather swallow poison than ever admit that to him.

"Joa, you're here. We are running late."

Joa snapped out of her fantasy to be confronted with reality and...wow, reality was damn fine. Ronan, wearing only a pair of black exercise shorts and sneakers, stood a few feet from her. Joa could see the fine sheen of perspiration on his shoulders, dampening his chest hair, which narrowed down into a fine line that bisected a very, very nice set of abs. His shorts hung low enough on his hips that she could see a stupendous pair of hip muscles, and Joa felt her knees weakening.

Wow.

Ronan gestured her into his kitchen. "Are you okay?" he asked, his hands on his hips. She wanted her hands there, her chest pressed into his, her tongue on the ball of his tan, freckled shoulder, tasting his skin.

Yeah, think about that, Jones. That's a marvelous way to take control of this situation.

Joa jammed her hands into the back pockets of her jeans—*so as not to touch you, my dear*—and met Ronan's eyes.

"Morning." *Excellent, Joa, you actually managed to croak a word.*

"Thanks for coming over so early. The kids are still asleep since they got to bed late last night. I battled with them and eventually put them into my bed with a movie. I also overslept and I'm running so late," Ronan said. "And I have a crazy day ahead of me."

"How so?" Joa asked, grateful for the neutral topic.

Was it her imagination or did Ronan seem too eager to respond to her innocuous question? "General madness at work, and I'll be home late tonight. I'm running a specialized sale on sports memorabilia."

Was he expecting her to start her duties as an au pair tonight? Could he possibly be that arrogant, that presumptuous? She'd come over this morning to discuss—and only discuss—Keely's wild suggestion, not to begin employment. She was here as a courtesy, that was all. She didn't want to be an au pair anymore—why did nobody seem to understand that?

"Keely might think she's boss of the world, but I saw your horrified face when she suggested you work for me. I know the situation isn't as cut-and-dried as she made it out to be," Ronan explained. "I made alternative arrangements for a babysitter tonight."

Joa arched her eyebrows, silently asking who'd agreed to help him out.

"My brother Finn is on monster duty tonight. Luckily, I should be done by ten."

Right. She remembered he was Murphy's chief auctioneer as well as being their worldwide operations manager. "I thought you only ran the big sales."

Ronan nodded. "Normally, I let the junior auctioneers run the smaller sales, but my sports guy was rushed to the hospital two days ago with a burst appendix. I do have other auctioneers, but there are some pretty big spenders in the audience so I thought I'd run the sale, connect with them on a guy-to-guy level."

"I'd like to see an auction," she admitted.

"You're always welcome, though I am assuming you will be at the auction for Isabel's collection. It will be one of the biggest auctions any house has conducted. It's been billed as a once-in-a-generation sale."

Oh, right. She'd temporarily forgotten that she and Keely had agreed to auction off their massive collection to swell the coffers of Isabel's foundation. The money raised would fund many projects in the greater Boston area, including the shelter Joa had found herself in fifteen years before.

Ronan shrugged, his expression self-deprecating. "So it's not a big deal or anything. Your lost Homer will be the last item auctioned, if Sadie manages to prove its provenance."

"Do you think it's genuine?"

"I would if I could." Ronan cursed and rubbed his hand over his jaw. "Look, I didn't mean to upset you…"

"I'm not upset, I'm annoyed," Joa replied. "Don't assume that I am one of those women who will use your kids to worm my way into your life. Yes, I'm attracted to you, but I've never thrown myself at a man in my life and you won't be the first. I'm not that desperate or that insecure."

She could, if she let herself, but she wouldn't. She had more pride than that.

Ronan crossed his arms over his chest and the muscles in his biceps bunched. Damn, he really wasn't helping.

"And if you don't want to be ogled then put on a shirt!" Joa added.

Ronan released another curse and stepped out from behind the counter to walk in the direction of the laundry room and yep, she couldn't miss it. His shorts were tented from a steel-hard erection. The bastard was lecturing her when he was equally affected.

"Seriously?" Joa nodded at his shorts. "That would suggest you are as attracted to me as I am to you."

He braked and closed his eyes. "Morning wood."

Joa wasn't buying it. "Don't BS me. You're equally tempted."

Why was she pushing this point when it would be smarter to ignore his reaction? What was wrong with her?

"You're a sexy woman and yeah, I'm attracted." He made it sound like he was admitting to a massive crime against humanity. "But it's still not going to happen," Ronan told her, his voice sharp.

"Damn straight it's not. I prefer my lovers to be excited about taking me to bed, not angry and resentful."

It was way past time to end the embarrassment and move on. "Let's simply admit that there's a mutual attraction that will never be acted on. Agreed?"

Ronan's reply was a sharp nod.

Ronan looked thoughtful as he rubbed the back of his neck, showing the pale skin of his underarm and sexy tufts of underarm hair. Man, she was losing it. She needed sex; she really did.

But not, obviously, with him.

Joa glanced away, feeling a small hint of guilt. It wasn't like her to refuse to help anyone—Isabel had taught her better—but Joa's gut instinct was to put a considerable amount of distance between her and Ronan. But she understood that working for him, helping him with his kids, would be a mental step backwards. Blowing air over her bottom lip, she looked at the photograph of his wife attached to his fridge by a heart-shaped magnet. Ronan was also, and obviously, still in love with his wife.

Going to work for him would be like flying from the frying pan into the fire.

She'd placed herself in this position before, working for men to whom she was attracted and it was time to stop repeating past mistakes.

Her previous employees had been nice men, good men, but she hadn't felt a fraction of the physical pull to them as she did to Ronan. Fighting that chemistry would be exhausting, but she was strong enough, had had enough practice at pushing down her emotions—the foster care system drummed that into you—that she could ignore this inconvenient attraction to Ronan Murphy with both her hands tied behind her back.

She would not put herself back into an uncomfortable, untenable, nobody-but-herself-to-blame situation. She had to look after herself first, just like she'd always been forced to do.

Joa stood up and reached for her bag, pulling it over her shoulder.

"I'm sorry, but no. I can't. I hope you find someone soon."

Ronan pushed his hands through his hair and looked horrified. Gobsmacked. Obviously, as a Murphy, he didn't hear the word *no* very often.

"What?"

"Best of luck, Ronan," Joa said, walking toward the back door. As she stepped into the sunroom, she turned and sent him a tight smile, drinking in that luscious body and doing her best to ignore his pissed-off expression.

"Oh, and if you don't want your female employees to lust after you then I strongly suggest you put on some clothes when conducting job interviews, Murphy. Walking around half-naked isn't conducive to keeping the arrangement businesslike and might give potential nannies the wrong impression."

Six

In the small office Carrick had allocated to her at Murphy's International, Sadie sat back in her chair and glared at her monitor. She had a ton of work to do, but she'd lost her ability to concentrate.

Carrick had strolled into her brain, plopped himself down and refused to leave.

Dammit.

Sadie pushed her laptop away and placed her arms on the desk, resting her chin on her fist. In a little more than a month her world had been flipped on its head, the plan of her life rewritten and reimagined.

Who knew that when she'd taken this job, a few scant weeks later she'd find herself pregnant and crazy obsessed over a man who made her blood sing?

Sadie thought back to her conversation with Hassan and, forcing herself to be as unemotional as possible, remembered his thoughtful comments on her situation. Was Carrick simply not good for Tamlyn or was he not good *to* her? Were Boston society's perceptions fair?

In Carrick, she'd seen no trace of the man who'd treated Tamlyn badly, who was verbally abusive, who thought the sun dimmed when he sat down.

Carrick was tough, sure—he had to be to run a multinational, successful business like Murphy's—and he took no prisoners, but so far, she hadn't seen the jerky man Tamlyn had told her about. Not in the way he spoke to his staff, his brothers, his friends.

Her.

Sadie sighed. Maybe she was *hoping* he wasn't the man Tamlyn and Beth said he was; maybe she wanted him to be a better version of himself with her; maybe she was seeing Carrick naively. He was the father of her unborn child, the man who took her from zero to horny in six seconds flat. It was natural for her to want to see the best in him.

And she couldn't help remembering that she'd also only seen the best side of Dennis before the wedding. It was only when they were back in Boston, juggling the demands of two successful careers, both traveling internationally, when the ugliness started to creep in.

Like all things, it had started small...

She desperately wanted to believe that Carrick wasn't another Dennis, that she wasn't misjudging him. Would Carrick also eventually turn out to be a bastard? If she believed Tamlyn and Beth, then he would.

If she had to trust her intuition, she believed he wouldn't.

But she'd trusted her intuition before and it had proved to be as faulty as a badly wired house.

Sadie rested her forehead on her bent arms, conscious of a headache building behind her eyes. She took a couple of deep breaths, felt her tension levels drop and told herself she was stressing about this for nothing. She wasn't going to marry Carrick, nor fall in love with him.

If he showed himself to be a bastard to her child, she'd make sure her baby was protected.

She wouldn't have these crazy thoughts running around her head if she hadn't slept with Carrick a second time. But she had to be honest here; she had no intention of *not* having sex with him in the immediate future.

Oh, she knew there would come a time when she'd feel too big, too uncomfortable, to think about sex, but that was half a year away. In less than a year, her life would be coated with an extra layer of crazy and she doubted that, between the baby and her job, she'd have the time to date, or have any interest in doing so.

Carrick would move on—why did that feel like acid splashing on her soul?—and she'd be a single mom wrestling her way through motherhood.

Until then she'd take this time, this reprieve, and do everything within reason that she wouldn't be able to do when she had the responsibility of a child.

And that included sleeping with, and not falling for, the very sexy Carrick Murphy.

"What are you frowning about?"

Sadie jerked her head up and looked toward the door. Think about the sexy devil and he arrives.

Sadie lifted a hand and sent him a quick smile. "Just general frustration."

"Baby or art-related?"

"Both," Sadie said as he leaned his shoulder into the door frame. His tie was pulled down from his open collar and lay flat against the white button-down shirt tucked into a pair of tailored pants.

Judging by his tired eyes and messy hair, the day had kicked his ass and she fought the urge to stand up and wrap her arms around his waist and hug him tight.

She suspected Carrick was the tree many people relied on for shelter from the sun, wind and rain, tall and broad and protective. But who protected him from the elements? Where did he lay his head?

"You look tired," Sadie said.

"Bitch of a day," he admitted, surprising her.

"Tell me." She didn't think he would, but miracles occasionally happened.

Carrick walked over to her small desk, picked up her cup of peppermint tea and, before she could warn him that it was hours old and stone cold, took a sip. Then he took another, draining the cup of its contents.

"One of the biggest items for the auction next week has been withdrawn."

"Why?"

Carrick pulled a face. "My client was told by his spirit guide that it wasn't a good time to sell, that he should wait for further instructions."

Sadie's mouth twitched. How bizarre. "You are making that up."

"Trust me, I'm not. Kookiness and cash are a volatile combination." Carrick sat on the edge of her desk and rubbed the back of his neck. "Our payroll system crashed so I've spent the afternoon yelling at the IT department to sort it out. And my PA is out sick and I'm spoiled. I don't like getting my own coffee."

Sadie knew that Marsha was his right-hand person and getting coffee was the least important thing she did for him. She organized his life and kept track of the million balls he had in the air. "Is she very ill? When will she be back at work?"

"God knows," Carrick replied, "since she has bronchitis and can't speak. She's been working from home and she's not very happy with me."

Sadie frowned. "Because you keep sending her work?"

Carrick shook his head. "No, because I had IT lock her out of the server so she can't work. It's the only way to make sure she gets some rest. Marsha is twice the workaholic I am."

Oh. That was sweet. And thoughtful. And very un-Dennis-like.

Sadie saw Ronan pass her open door, watched him brake and backtrack. He flashed her a smile—holy smokes, these Murphy men were all birthed by angels—and did that leaning into the door frame thing tall men did so well.

"I was just coming to find you," Ronan told Carrick.

"Problem?" Carrick asked, rubbing his temples with his index fingers.

"Always," Ronan said, almost cheerfully. Carrick cursed and Sadie saw the concerned look Ronan threw his way. The brothers were tight and seeing their bond made her feel emotional and a little lost.

It made her miss her family.

"Can you handle it?" Carrick asked him. "If there's something I can help with let me know. Preferably tomorrow."

"Will do." Ronan nodded. "I'm going for a drink at the Pig and Plough. Would you two like to join me?"

"Who has the kids?" Carrick asked.

"Finn said he needed some uncomplicated company and offered to spend the afternoon with them. They talked him into taking them to that massive pet store across town."

These brothers had each other's backs and Sadie couldn't help but feel envious. The same could not be said of her siblings…

Then Ronan grinned and he looked ten years younger, free and happy. "He sent me a video of the boys in puppy heaven."

Ronan pulled out his phone, swiped his thumb across it and handed it to Carrick. Carrick angled the phone so that she could see the large screen, and she smiled at the video clip of the two little boys sitting in a pen full of Siberian Husky puppies. They were laughing uncontrollably as puppies ate their hair, licked their faces and gnawed on their trainers.

Carrick laughed and looked at his brother. "Newsflash, they are going to nag you incessantly about getting a dog until you give in."

Sadie stirred the pot. "They won't settle for one. They'll each want their own."

"If they make my kids happy, I'll buy them a dozen." He looked at Carrick. "Where did you get Jazz from? Damn, that was a great dog."

Jazz? Sadie frowned. She'd heard that name before. Oh, right, it was the name of the dog that had been such a bone of contention during his and Tamlyn's divorce. Carrick had resolved the argument over custody by having the dog put down.

Sadie didn't understand how he could kill a dog to resolve an argument.

"Actually, I found him at a no-kill shelter," Carrick replied.

Ronan frowned, confused. "But he had papers. He was highly pedigreed. Tamlyn told us he had a family tree longer than ours."

Carrick's mouth twisted. "Jazz was a mutt. A lovely mutt, but still a mutt." Sadie noticed that Carrick didn't try to explain or excuse Tamlyn's lies; he just stated his truth, calmly and precisely.

She needed to know. She had to know. "Can I ask you a question?"

Carrick looked at her and slowly nodded.

"Why did you euthanize Jazz?"

For a long moment Sadie thought he wasn't going to answer but his answer, when it finally came, was short and to the point. "Jazz had cancer of the bowel. Tamlyn, to give her credit, loved that dog, but she wouldn't face the fact that he was suffering and in pain. I did the kindest thing."

"But she—"

Behind Carrick's head, she saw Ronan's quick shake of his head, his fierce frown. She stopped talking. It didn't matter what Tamlyn had said. Sadie now had Carrick's version of that event and it was diametrically opposite to what she'd believed.

Carrick's eyes, when they met hers, were as hard as stone and twice as icy. "Care to tell me how you heard that story about my dog? Because that was one of the few things that didn't make the social columns."

Carrick really didn't care what the world thought about his marriage, how the members of A-list Boston society viewed him. The people he cared about knew him for who he was. They were aware of how he'd conducted himself during his marriage. His siblings and his close friends knew he could be impatient and demanding, but they also knew he was never abusive or cruel.

Yes, his marriage had bombed. But the stories that were out there were not based on anything remotely resembling the truth. And Sadie, judging by the fact that she'd heard about Jazz, knew more than most.

And, if he wasn't mistaking the confusion in her eyes, she'd believed what she heard.

Carrick felt sick to his stomach. He could see it in her eyes, in her white fingers clutching her biceps. The mother of his unborn child had doubts about his character, was uncertain about how he would treat her going forward.

For the first time his urge to explain was almost stronger than his pride.

Almost, but not quite.

Carrick waited for Ronan to leave before starting with the easiest of the dozen questions he had. "How did you hear about Jazz?"

Sadie pushed her top teeth into her bottom lip. When he didn't speak again, she sighed and his anger climbed. Tamlyn had been out of his life for five years but she was still causing havoc.

"Beth, your ex-wife's—"

"I know who Beth is," Carrick interrupted her.

"Well, Beth is a virtual assistant and I am one of her clients, her main client. She's also an old friend."

Carrick closed his eyes, feeling sick. Behind Tamlyn, Beth was the biggest spreader of Tamlyn vs Carrick rumors and instantly believed anything vicious her older sister said. If Sadie and Beth were friends, God knows what lies she would've told Sadie.

"I'm also friends with Tamlyn."

Oh, yeah, this was just getting more fabulous by the minute. "Well, then, you got it straight from the horse's mouth."

Never mind that the horse was spouting BS.

"Care to tell me why you never informed me about your connection to my ex-wife?"

Sadie held his hard stare. "I didn't think it was germane to the situation."

The hell it wasn't. Sadie pushed her hair off her shoulders and straightened her spine. "I only heard one side of the story, Carrick. I haven't heard yours."

"And you are never going to."

Sadie's eyebrows pulled together and her mouth thinned. "Well, then I— People are going to keep believing her side of the story."

"People can think what they want. I have no control over that."

"Of course you do. You can push back. You can refute her allegations. You can tell your side of the story."

"My side of the story? How old are we, ten?" Carrick scoffed. "My marriage is over. I never talk about it and I don't owe anyone a damn explanation."

Hurt and annoyance flashed in her eyes. "Not even me?"

Especially not her. He wanted—no, he *needed*—her to believe him, without proof, without thought. He needed her to know him, to make up her own mind, to discard what she'd heard and trust him, dammit.

They were going to be in each other's lives for a long time and as the mother of his child, she was going to be one of the most important people in his life. He needed her to see him without the filter of other people's perceptions.

And if she couldn't, then this road was going to be long, ugly and as bumpy as hell.

"Make up your own mind about me, Sadie," Carrick told her, exhausted and not a little defeated.

"There are reasons that it's easy for me to believe her, Carrick," Sadie quietly stated.

He didn't care. Her reasons didn't matter...

He needed her faith.

He needed her to decide, to know, on a fundamental level, he wasn't the man Tamlyn or Beth made him out to be.

He would never settle for anything less. And he'd never, ever explain.

When the rumors started circling, his family and close friends instinctively closed ranks, their trust in him unshakeable. He'd been grateful and touched and their reaction was now the standard he set for all his relationships.

Carrick rubbed his forehead, his headache pushing against his skull. He hadn't had a migraine since leaving Tamlyn and it made sense that talking about his ex would bring one on.

As always, taking a hammer to his head sounded like an appropriate solution.

When Carrick's house was full of people, it felt like a home, not a conglomeration of rooms, most of which he didn't use. With voices and laughter reigning through the historic Beacon Hill house, Carrick felt like his dad had just stepped out of the room and that his stepmom, Raeni, was in the kitchen, whipping up one of her lethal cocktails.

His nephews were playing with a box of his old

LEGO pieces on the Oriental carpet on the far side of the room, and conversation rose and fell. It felt like old times. Carrick watched his nephews for a minute, his heart spluttering at the thought that in a few years, it would be his kid on the carpet playing with cars or blocks or dolls. And he couldn't wait.

Carrick looked across the room to where Sadie was talking to Levi's sisters, Jules and Darby, his eyes dropping to her still-flat stomach. He hadn't seen her since their conversation about his past two days ago. He'd been out of town.

When he heard that Tanna was back in Boston with Levi, he'd made arrangements for this impromptu get-together from New York via Marsha, and he'd called Sadie and suggested she join them. He'd missed her, dammit.

Before responding to his invitation, Sadie, as forthright as ever, immediately addressed their argument.

"Are you still mad because I didn't tell you about Beth and Tamlyn?"

He wasn't crazy about the connection, but there was damn all he could do about it. "No."

"Have you changed your mind about talking to me about her?" Sadie asked.

Talk about Tamlyn? The world had to end first. "No."

She'd dropped a quiet "okay," but hadn't made a commitment to attending tonight so he'd been surprised, and ridiculously happy, to see her walk into his house earlier that evening. Then she'd removed her coat to reveal her super-short, A-line black cocktail dress, embellished with pearls and the black lace sleeves ending three quarters down her slim arms.

Then he'd fought the urge to carry her up to his bedroom.

It was official: he couldn't resist her...dammit.

Carrick pulled himself back to the present and looked around the room. Finn stood in the corner, talking to Mason and Ronan, who wasn't paying any attention to their conversation. Carrick followed his gaze and saw that he was looking at Joa Jones. Then Ronan's eyes dropped to his kids, and Joa's eyes left Sam and Aron to look at Ro.

Well, well, well... Wasn't that interesting?

Carrick felt movement next to him and looked down at his sister. He pulled her to his side. "You and Levi look so happy, Tanna. I'm so glad you are back in Boston, that you are joining us at Murphy's and that I'm going to get to boss you around daily."

Tanna stuck her tongue out at him. "You can try."

She wrapped her arms around his waist, the way she used to when she was a little girl. Carrick felt his throat close and he rested his head against hers. He'd raised her with the help of his brothers from the time she was ten and she'd been his to protect. Now she had Levi and he could stop worrying about her.

But a part of him always would. She was his kid, dammit, as well as his sister. And now he got to raise a child from the beginning. He was going to love and protect and raise a baby of his own.

How utterly cool and exciting and nerve-racking was that?

Carrick kissed her hair, released her and stepped back. "Enjoy your welcome home party, Tan."

Tanna handed him a wobbly, emotional smile, but before she could respond, Levi simultaneously slapped a hand on Carrick's shoulder and snagged Tanna's waist, hauling her to his side. Levi dropped a hard, openmouthed kiss on his sister's mouth and Carrick made a show of staring at the high, molded hundred-year-old ceiling.

"You can look now, Carrick," Tanna said, laughing.

Carrick met his amused friend's eyes. "He's going to be a pain in the ass about this, isn't he, honey?" Levi said.

"Indubitably," Tanna replied.

Levi placed a kiss on Tanna's temple. "Can I have a word with your brother, Tan?"

Tanna nodded and drifted away. When she was out of earshot, Carrick raised his eyebrows at his friend, enjoying the heat in Levi's cheeks. Levi was the most composed, centered guy he knew and it was fun to watch him rock on his heels, his shoulders hunching as he jammed his hands into the front pockets of his jeans.

"Um, I'd normally ask your dad this, but—you know."

Carrick pretended he had no idea what was coming next. "What are you talking about? And, hey, did you catch the game last night?"

"No, I, Carrick, listen…uh…"

"It was crap. The ref was biased."

"Dammit, Carrick, I'm trying to say something here!" Levi snapped, visibly annoyed.

"Something that's more important than the game?" Carrick teased him, but took a step back, just in case Levi lost it and punched him.

"Can I marry your sister or not?" Levi demanded, impatient.

Oh, this was far too good an opportunity to pass up. Carrick grinned, saw the relief in Levi's eyes. "Not."

Levi's mouth fell open, caught totally off guard. His eyes bugged out and his pupils turned a startling shade of red. "Okay, thanks for nothing. Just so you know, nothing but death will stop us from getting married this time around."

Carrick lifted his hands and rapidly backtracked. "Whoa, calm down. I was only joking." Carrick risked putting his hand on Levi's shoulder and giving it a tight squeeze. "You know that I approve. I approved when she was nineteen, I totally approve now. Not that you need my approval."

Levi's tension levels dropped and Carrick thought he was on firmer ground. "Good to know." Levi nailed him with a hard stare. "And that was a lousy stunt to pull."

"It was fun until you got this rabid look in your eyes," Carrick said.

He held out his hand and when Levi's hand met his, he pulled his friend into a one-armed hug. "Congratulations, man. I'm genuinely happy for you."

"Thanks," Levi said, now sporting a wide grin.

Nope, he wasn't done with his about-to-be brother-in-law just yet. "So, one down, two to go."

Levi pulled his eyes off Tanna to frown at Carrick. "What do you mean?"

"I'm giving you my blessing but you need Ronan's and Finn's, too," Carrick told him, thinking that yanking Levi's chain was the best fun he'd had in ages. "They helped raise Tanna. I think it's only fair you ask them, too."

"You do realize that I don't actually need their permission?" Levi grumbled, sending Ronan an anxious look.

Carrick swallowed his smile. "I do, but Ronan and Finn take their responsibility to our sister very seriously."

Levi released a curse and stomped across the room to where Ronan was standing. Carrick saw him jerk his head to Finn, a silent request that he join them. Carrick finally allowed his laughter to escape.

Sadie touched his elbow and raised her eyebrows at him. "What are you up to, Carrick Murphy?"

Carrick's eyes traced her delicate features and he saw the curiosity in her bright blue eyes.

It was strange that she immediately picked up that he was messing with Levi; many wouldn't. Very few people had, over the years, managed to read him and he mentally squirmed. It unnerved him that she could.

Since Sadie still seemed to be waiting for an answer, he lifted one shoulder. "Levi asked for permission to marry Tanna. I felt it my duty to give him a hard time."

Sadie rolled her eyes. "Men. *Honestly*."

"He'll probably announce their engagement to-night."

Sadie shifted from one foot to the other. "That's wonderful. But I can't help thinking that I shouldn't be here, that I'm crashing this party."

Carrick lowered his voice. "The moment you conceived my child you became part of this family. They might not know it yet, but I do. You have every right to be here."

Sadie looked like she had her doubts, but instead of arguing, she looked across the room to where Levi stood with Tanna's brothers. Carrick followed her gaze and noticed how Levi's gaze wandered over to Tanna and when her eyes met his, the sexual energy arcing between them threatened to blister the paint on the walls.

"Holy smokes, hand me a fan," Sadie muttered.

Carrick groaned.

"There are some things an older brother does not need to see," Carrick muttered, turning his back on his sister and Levi. "She was ten, like, *yesterday*."

Carrick felt Sadie's hand slide into his and his bumping heart settled, then sighed. What was it about this woman that made him feel relaxed and energized and horny?

Carrick tugged Sadie toward the drinks table and after offering her a virgin mojito, he poured himself a whiskey. Sadie murmured her thanks and sipped her drink. "It must have been as scary as all hell, having the responsibility of a ten-year-old."

It had been and Carrick didn't mind admitting it. "It was, but what other choice did we have? Somehow, between us, at twenty, nineteen and eighteen, we made it work."

"What about school and dating and, you know, having a life?"

Carrick thought back, able to clearly remember his sister as a little girl and the day-to-day grind. "We came up with a system. I dropped out of college to work full-time at Murphy's. Luckily, we had an amazing management team who looked after the company until I was old enough and experienced enough to run it myself. Ronan and Finn finished college and joined me when they were done."

"I'm sorry you didn't get to finish school, Carrick."

It wasn't that big a deal. Yeah, sometimes he thought he might like a certificate on the wall, but he'd learned all he knew through workplace experience, books and the management team, and he thought he was doing okay. He hadn't killed the company yet. In fact, they'd had one of their best years ever.

"You must've been out of your mind with worry when you heard about her accident."

The worst night of his life. Carrick took a sip of his whiskey and stared down into his glass. He shuddered, remembering his panic, those anxious hours waiting to hear if she'd make it and meeting Levi for the first time. "Levi was the first person on the scene and he visited her while she was in the hospital. Somewhere along the way they fell in love."

"But they are only getting together now?"

"They got engaged back then but Tanna was so young. She dumped him a few days before the wedding," Carrick explained.

Sadie smiled at the happy couple. "I don't think that's going to happen again."

"It had better damn well not," Carrick growled. "The last non-wedding cost me a frigging fortune."

"You don't really care about the money." Sadie slipped her hand into his and squeezed his fingers. "You're an awesome brother, Carrick. I can see that she adores you."

She bent her head to look down at their linked fingers. "Thank you for inviting me tonight. It's been a long time since I attended a family gathering." She looked momentarily embarrassed. "I travel a lot and I don't often attend family gatherings. Well, except for Hassan's family, obviously."

Carrick saw the tenderness in her eyes, heard the soft note in her voice. And cursed when jealousy scoured his throat.

"And who exactly is he?" Carrick asked through gritted teeth.

Sadie sipped her drink and looked at him through long and dark and thick eyelashes. Yeah, that coquettish look was designed to melt irritation at fifty paces.

"Hassan is Prince Hassan Ramid El-Aboud. I was with him in Abu Dhabi when you asked me to consult on the Homer."

With him? Was she with him *naked*? She needed

to define *with him* and she needed to do it quickly. "Explain." Carrick bit the word out.

"Well, there was talk about us getting married," Sadie blithely replied, and Carrick felt the pressure in his head expand.

"He's asked you to marry him?"

Sadie sipped her mojito. "Uh-huh…"

She was having his kid and was blithely talking about marriage to someone else? Oh, hell no! "Are you being serious?"

"Sure. His family loves me and I've been to two of his sister's weddings and his parents' fortieth wedding anniversary celebration. Hassan is the only son and he's spoiled rotten. They can't wait to marry him off."

"And they've chosen you? An American non-Muslim?"

"His mom is British and they love me."

"And have you told him that you are pregnant with my child?" Carrick demanded, trying to keep his voice low, but unable to mask his fury.

"Sure," Sadie cheerfully told him. She lifted her shoulders and let them fall in a careless shrug. "Hassan's fine with it. Excited, even."

"You're not going to marry him and he's not raising my child!" Carrick roared and every one of his guests whipped around, their eyes wide.

Sadie gurgled with laughter. Carrick huffed. Well, that was one hell of a way to tell the world there was going to be another Murphy—God help them all—in eight or so months' time. Lucky for them, their friends and family knew how to keep a secret.

Sadie's smirk had him wondering what, exactly, she was up to.

"I…what…*dammit*."

Sadie winked at Levi. "He can hand it out, but he's not so good at taking it."

Levi walked over to them and held out his big fist for her to bump and Sadie tapped her knuckles against his. Then she turned back to Carrick and shook her head.

"I was messing with you, Carrick, just like you messed with Levi earlier. And no, I'm not going to marry Hassan, not now, not ever. While his family does think I'm fabulous, they know, as do Hassan and I, that we will never be anything more than friends. You're looking a bit pale. Would you like to lie down?"

He placed his hands on her cheeks, captured her face between his palms and laughed against her lips.

This woman, she was going to drive him mad.

Going to? Nope, it was already happening.

Seven

In the hallway of Carrick's house, Sadie pulled on her coat and was winding her scarf around her neck when Carrick touched her elbow. She turned, and he pulled her to the side, dropping his head to speak in her ear.

"Stay."

One word, so powerful.

He moved off to say goodbye to his other guests, and Sadie stared at his broad back, needing to go but wanting to stay. If she didn't follow his friends and family out the door, there was a good chance she'd end up in Carrick's bed again and the line between sex and affection, desire and, well, not love but liking, would become more blurred.

She could not, would not, fall in love with Carrick. She'd fallen in love once before and it had hurt like hell.

She could do friendship, she could do sex, she could do coparenting, but handing her heart over was a step too far. But the more time she spent with Carrick, the blurrier that line became. And those lines were smudged enough already because she was starting to believe that Carrick was nothing like the guy Tamlyn and Beth had portrayed him to be.

There…

She'd admitted it. And it scared her half to death because it felt like she was ripping down a barrier between them, an essential means of protection.

She really should go. But instead of walking through the door, she shrugged out of her coat, hung it up on the hook and tucked her scarf back into the side pocket.

She wasn't going anywhere…

Not tonight anyway.

Sadie walked back down the hallway. As she passed the dining room, complete with a sixteen-seater table and chairs and an elegant chandelier, she saw the gilded frame of a massive painting hanging over the fireplace. Unable to resist the lure of an exceptional piece of art, she slipped inside the room and walked past the tall chairs to stand in front of the painting, her eyes flying over the image of Madonna and child.

She didn't recognize the artist, but she did recognize the style, Venetian, possibly eighteenth century. In the style of Caravaggio…possibly by one of his followers because there was no way that Carrick Murphy could have a real Caravaggio on his dining room wall.

Could he?

Sadie heard the tread of masculine feet and when they stopped at the door, she turned her head to look at Carrick. She jerked her head at the painting and gave him a wry smile. "I'm debating whether this is a real Caravaggio or not."

Carrick smiled. "Not. It's by one of his apprentices, we're not sure which one, but we're sure it's not by the master."

"It's still amazingly emotive." Sadie pointed at the face of the Madonna, her face suffused with love for her newborn child. "She's beautiful. They both are."

"The mother-child bond," Carrick said, coming to stand next to her, his hands in the pockets of his black pants. "It's a universal theme."

Sadie placed her hand on the back of one of the tall dining chairs and kept her eyes on the serene face of the Madonna. "Do you remember your real mom?"

Carrick tensed, but he eventually nodded. "A little. I was six when she died and I remember her reading a book, something about a bear hunt."

The book had been a favorite of hers, too.

"I remember her perfume, that she loved to hug, how pale she was when she got sick."

"How did she die?" Sadie asked him, keeping her voice soft and nondemanding.

"Cancer," Carrick replied. "She was diagnosed in January and was gone by April."

Sadie winced; that was very quick indeed. "And when did your stepmom enter your lives?"

"I was eight," Carrick replied, his expression softening. "She gathered us all up and made us feel… I don't know how to explain it, safe? Loved? Complete?"

"My dad, he tried but he wasn't very good at the day-to-day practicalities of raising us. He didn't know how to deal with three heartbroken, confused little boys." Carrick's expression was pure guilt. "I shouldn't say that. He did the best he could while dealing with his own grief."

"You weren't criticizing your dad, Carrick, just stating a fact." Sadie soothed him, placing her hand on his biceps. Carrick covered her hand with his and squeezed her fingers.

"Raeni had this enormous heart, and a deep capacity to love. We were so lucky Dad met and married her." Carrick looked around and grimaced. "It's pretty cold in here. Let's go back to the reception room. Or the study."

Sadie followed him out of the room and touched the frame of a sketch hanging opposite the door. "I'd love a cup of tea, actually."

Carrick changed direction and led her down the hallway to the expansive gourmet kitchen, its surfaces covered with glasses and dinner plates.

Sadie winced at the mess. "Shall we pack your dishwasher?"

Carrick filled the kettle and put it on the stove. "My cleaning service will deal with it the morning."

He opened the cupboard and frowned at the boxes of tea. "I have about ten different types and I'm not sure why since I never drink the stuff." He motioned her over. "Pick your poison."

Sadie decided on chamomile and watched as Carrick tossed water over the bag. He held her cup and gestured for her to follow him and she did, scooting around the island and heading for a small nook situated just off the kitchen. He placed her cup on the coffee table and gestured to the wide, comfy-looking blue-and-white-striped sofa. On the wall opposite was a widescreen TV. Sadie sat down, and Carrick slumped down next to her, kicking off his shoes and placing his feet on the coffee table.

"I'm so happy Tanna is coming back to live in Boston and that she's going to marry Levi. It's a long time overdue."

"I think things happen when they are supposed to. Maybe the timing was wrong for them back then and right for them now." Sadie picked up her cup and wrapped her hands around its warm surface. "You said they met and fell in love while she was recovering from her accident?"

Carrick leaned back, shifted down in the sofa and rested his head on the back. "Yeah. She was nineteen and she had some pretty extensive injuries." His green eyes were haunted. "That night was probably one of the worst of my life. And the months after that weren't any fun, either. Tamlyn helped me get through that horrible period." He pulled a face. "She was pretty amazing, to be honest. She kept me from going off my head."

Sadie ignored the flash of jealousy dancing along her nerves. "I'm glad she was there for you." And she was; nobody should go through something so horrible on their own.

"Funny to think that we were all with our wives back then, although none of us were married," Carrick said, his voice rumbly with exhaustion. "Ronan was with Thandi, Finn with Beah. They'd met a few months before. Within the year we were all married. And none of our marriages worked out. Raeni would've hated that. She'd hate to know that, ten years on, we're all emotionally scarred, and all so damn scared of getting it wrong again."

"Aren't we all?" Sadie murmured. "Getting divorced dents your confidence big-time."

Carrick rolled his head to look at her. "You were married?"

"Yep."

"How long did yours last?"

"Three years," Sadie said before raising her cup to her lips.

Carrick half turned, his attention on her. "What happened?"

Sadie wanted to push away his question, to change the subject because she hated talking about Dennis, explaining how she'd failed. She should never have said yes. Not to dating him, sleeping with him, to their engagement and certainly not to their marriage.

But she could tell Carrick; she was sure she could.

And maybe then he'd understand why she'd believed what she'd heard about his past.

"I was warned about him," she softly admitted, telling him the secret that no one else knew, not even Hassan. It was something she'd intended to take to the grave but here she was, telling Carrick.

"Who warned you?"

Sadie put her cup down and bent to pull off her strappy heels. Pulling her feet up onto the edge of the sofa, she wrapped her arms around her bent knees. "Back then I was working for an art gallery on Charles Street and I was locking up when I saw this woman waiting for me. She asked me if we could talk and I said okay, so we walked to a coffee shop across the road."

Carrick placed his hand on her knee and Sadie felt some of the knots in her neck unraveling.

"What did she say?"

"That he was abusive and controlling and that he wasn't a nice guy," Sadie answered. "She was with him for a few years. She thought they were going to get married but he made promises he never kept."

"Did you believe her?"

Sadie shook her head. "He wasn't like that with me, not then. I mentioned it to Dennis and he said she didn't take their breakup well, that he never made her any promises and that she was a bit unstable."

"And you loved him and wanted to believe him."

Yeah, she had. "And he was the perfect boyfriend. On our honeymoon he was the perfect husband. It was only when we returned to the city that things started falling apart."

"She told me not to marry him, and she was right. I should've listened to her," Sadie added.

"A stranger who just appeared out of the blue and started talking trash about your man?" Carrick lifted his eyebrows. "If you had a hint that he was a bastard, then I'd say yeah, you could've listened to her, but at that time he was making you happy. Why would you believe her?"

She'd told herself the same thing, in a hundred different ways, but it felt so good to hear her own rationalizations coming from his lips. "Because I didn't believe her, and because nobody believed me when I said my ex was abusive and controlling, I tend to over-believe what women say about their men."

Carrick sat up slowly, his eyes fixed on her face. "So that's why you instinctively believed everything bad you heard about me?"

Sadie nodded slowly. "Have you ever not been believed, Carrick?" Then Sadie remembered that he'd never explained his view of his marriage. He simply didn't put himself in the position of needing to be being believed or questioned.

Sadie plowed on.

"I told my family. They said I was exaggerating. My dad said I was being melodramatic and my mom agreed. The day after I told them how bad my marriage was, how awful Dennis was to me, my dad accepted tickets to watch a Red Sox game with him. I told my sister, only to later hear that she and my mom had long conversations about me, trying to work out how they could get me to see a psychologist. They staged an intervention, saying I was obviously troubled. And not thinking straight."

Carrick stared at her, horrified.

Sadie rested her chin on her knee and Carrick gripped her ankle. Sadie instantly felt calmer and more grounded. "I told some friends, but somehow my words always got back to Dennis and the abuse intensified. Our friends started to shun me, my own friends didn't believe me and my family wanted me to get psychological help. But I still went back to them. I still kept trying to drink from that well. And every time they dismissed my feelings, every time they defended Dennis, I felt like I was reexperiencing the emotional abuse."

"I'm so sorry, Sadie."

"I haven't spoken to any of my family since the divorce," Sadie admitted.

Carrick's hand briefly tightened on her ankle. "Your choice or theirs?"

"Both, I suppose. I never contacted them after the papers were signed and they've never reached out, either. I've heard that Dennis still stays in contact with them, that he's a frequent visitor to my parents' and siblings' houses. He spent last Thanksgiving with them."

"He hijacked your family. And your friends," Carrick said, and Sadie heard the anger in his voice. He met her eyes and she saw the buzz of fury in that light gaze. "Seriously, the guy needs to have his features rearranged and I'd be happy to do it."

Sadie smiled. Call her bloodthirsty, but she'd love to see that.

Carrick's expression turned pensive. "Maybe you should reach out to your family, Sadie. Check in to let them know you are fine."

She'd thought about doing that, especially since she had a child on the way, but she was scared. Didn't she have a right to be? She'd been disappointed by her family so often that she didn't want to admit she was pregnant from a one-night stand and going to be a single mother.

She was already the black sheep; this news would upgrade her to scarlet status.

But as much as she wished she could treat their reaction lightly, seeing their disappointment would just be another deep rip in a spirit that had yet to heal.

Why do that to herself? No, it was easier to keep her distance, to assume they were disappointed in her rather than confront them and have their disappointment confirmed.

"I'm sorry no one believed you, Sades," Carrick said, his voice a deep rumble. "I promise to always—"

Sadie held up her hand, her slashing movements cutting off his words. "Please don't promise something you can't deliver, Carrick." Her voice cracked. "I couldn't bear it."

Carrick ran his hand over her hair, down the back of her neck. "I'm going to do my best not to disappoint you, Sadie."

At another time in her life, in another incarnation, those words would've caused a warm fire in her belly. Today, here and now, it terrified her to think he'd be yet another person who kicked and bruised her heart.

That battered organ couldn't withstand any more abuse.

Sadie, her head on Carrick's chest, lifted her eyes to the painting above her head and released an annoyed sigh. Despite spending more hours on researching the painting than she should, she was still no closer to discovering who the artist was or why it felt so familiar.

For someone who prided herself on her extensive knowledge about art and artists, the puzzle was deeply frustrating.

"Welcome to my world," Carrick said, his hand sliding down her bare back.

"What's that?" Sadie asked, unable to pull her eyes from the painting. Who else used those tiny splashes of red, the flash of a reflection in the water, the hint of yellow in the sky?

"That painting will drive you nuts," Carrick told her, amusement coating every word. "Just accept that you will never know who painted it or why."

"Not happening," Sadie told him. Dropping her head, she looked at the smiling face of the naked man she lay on top of. Stretching, she brushed her lips against his, her nipples dragging across his chest. Sadie liked the fact that his eyes went foggy so she did it again and Carrick's fingers dug into the skin on her butt.

Yeah, waking up with Murphy was a spectacular way to start the day.

Sadie drew circles on his chest with her fingers. Last night they'd delved into her past, her murky marriage, but his past had been off-limits.

He still wasn't prepared to explain...

She'd exposed herself last night, rolled away the boulder to allow him to look inside her carefully concealed cave, but Carrick had given her nothing. He still refused to speak about Tamlyn or their marriage.

But did it matter? Did Sadie need him to? Whatever happened between him and his ex had nothing to do with her, and while she would never condone abuse of any kind, she was adult enough to know that some women didn't always tell the truth.

Carrick wasn't anything like Tamlyn had portrayed him. He wasn't the jerk, the arrogant, derisive man she'd described.

He was confident, he didn't suffer fools, but he wasn't cruel. Or selfish. Or ugly.

He loved his family, he was ethical in his business practices and he treated everyone he met, from janitors to wealthy clients, with respect. Sadie couldn't imagine him treating his wife with anything less than the respect he automatically gave others.

She wasn't going to speculate as to why Tamlyn spread rumors about Carrick—anger over being rejected, a need for revenge?—Sadie just knew that Tamlyn had lied.

She'd trusted Tamlyn's version because nobody had believed Sadie's. Sadie now knew that she'd misplaced that trust, that she'd believed something because she'd wanted to believe it.

And because, God, this was hard to admit, it didn't make her feel quite as much of an idiot, quite so alone, knowing that Tamlyn—so smart—had also had a mess of a marriage.

Sadie had also wanted to believe he was a bastard in his marriage because it placed a barrier between him and her, a wall her heart couldn't climb. But time spent with Carrick dissolved that wall...

Dennis hadn't shown his true colors until much later in their relationship; maybe Carrick would do the same...

Sadie shook her head, her fingers digging into Carrick's skin. No, that was just her mind playing tricks on her, wanting her to be safe, protected. Her heart knew that, with Carrick, she was safe, she was protected. He wouldn't let anyone hurt her, including himself.

Peace, warm and soft, rolled over her, and Sadie released an enormous sigh, every inch of her body going lax as she surrendered to the truth. She trusted Carrick, a surprise when she thought she'd never trust anyone again.

But she was also going to have a baby with Carrick and he was going to be in her life for a long time. She might be on that slippery slope sliding into love, but he didn't love her—there was no law that stated if you loved someone they had to love you back. And since she wasn't sixteen, she knew the difference between sex and love and she had no illusions that sleeping together meant anything more than mutual attraction.

If she couldn't stop herself from falling in love with him—and she intended to try to stop herself—she'd have to hide her love for him. She would never be that woman who would do or say or be anything to get a man to love her.

She'd done that before. She'd lost herself in pursuit of love, and she categorically refused to do that again.

Carrick felt Sadie's breath against his skin, felt her narrow chest rising and falling, and wondered what she was thinking about. He glanced down and saw the frown between her eyebrows, the tension in her mouth. He swallowed down the offer to help her figure it out.

Did he want to go there? Did he want to dive deeper?

They'd already covered a lot of emotional ground last night and he didn't know if he wanted to cover more. He needed to keep her at arm's length emotionally, not physically. He simply couldn't stomach losing another woman he loved.

He'd loved his mom, and she'd died. He'd loved Raeni, and ditto. Tamlyn, he'd loved as much as he could at the time, and she'd messed with his head and his reputation.

He could not afford to repeat past mistakes, because it hurt too damn much.

And he and Sadie had to keep their heads on

straight. Their child would be the bridge between them and if they allowed their emotions to become involved, if he and Sadie fell out, their child would suffer.

He refused to allow that to happen.

So no. Just no. They had to keep this simple.

Sex they could handle; love was a biological weapon.

"I love your skin," Carrick said, wanting to remind them both that loving her body was as far as he was prepared to go.

"I love you touching my skin," Sadie replied, her voice dropping to a sexy murmur. He was sure she didn't realize that her voice deepened when she was aroused.

She could recite the most boring text in that sexy voice and he'd be hard in, like, two seconds.

As he was right now.

And Sadie knew it because she lifted her knee and ran it up and down his shaft. She ran her hand across his abs and over his rib cage, spreading tiny prickles of delight across his skin. For the longest time, foreplay had been a means to a happy ending, but touching Sadie, being caressed by her, was something he could do even without the earth-shattering orgasm at the end of it.

Of course, since he was a guy, he preferred it to end with its natural, satisfying conclusion.

Rolling out from under her, Carrick rested his head in his hand and asked Sadie to roll onto her back. She did so without any shyness, revealing her naked body to his hungry eyes. Her breasts were perfectly round, her nipples a sexy pink. Her stomach was still flat and sometimes he forgot that his child was growing inside her, that beneath the layers of muscle and skin, a little human carrying his genes was, hopefully, flourishing.

Carrick sat up and bent his head to drop a kiss on her stomach, just below her navel, wanting a small connection between himself and the child he'd played a part in creating.

Then Sadie's scent, warm and musky and aroused, drifted up to him and Carrick forgot about babies and pregnancy, his thoughts moving on to how quickly he could have Sadie on the edge of orgasm.

He knew he could straddle her now. He could slide into her and she'd welcome his weight, but he wanted to go slow, to treat her like she was infinitely precious and wonderful.

Carrick ran his hand over her mons, lifting his head to suck a nipple, pulling it against the roof of his mouth. Sadie's back arched and he felt her hands in his hair and heard her breathy moans, looking for more.

Expecting him to give it to her... .

Beneath him, her knees fell apart, her legs shifting to accommodate him, and he smiled, loving the fact that Sadie wanted him as much as he wanted her. But this morning he needed to go slow, to nibble and suck and tease.

Carrick's mouth drifted down her sternum, did a detour over her rib cage and he dipped his tongue into her belly button, loving the little swirl of skin. Placing his hands on the inside of her thighs, holding her legs apart, he placed his nose on her strip of skin, inhaling her essence—salty, sweet, all Sadie.

He moved down, but ignored her lifted hips, holding her thighs so that he remained in control. Enjoying her soft skin under his fingertips, he ran his tongue down the ridge between femininity and her thigh, smiling at her frustrated growl.

He knew what she wanted, what she needed, but he now knew her well enough to push her, to make her wait, to build her up so she would shatter.

And he wanted her to do that on his tongue, in his mouth...

Carrick swiped his tongue over her and Sadie launched herself up, pushing herself into his mouth, demanding more, demanding all he had. He rubbed his lips across her, sucking that small bundle of nerves and lifting his hands up to cover her breasts, to pull her nipples into hard points. She was the one who was being pleasured but it was he who couldn't get enough; he who was insatiable. He felt Sadie's fingers tugging his hair and, knowing that she was close, sucked her gently and felt her shiver.

Every muscle in her body contracted as tremors rushed over her skin. Wanting to give her more, he sucked her again and she screamed.

And groaned. And called his name.

Yeah, job well-done, Carrick thought as he crawled up her to rest his weight on the forearms he placed on either side of her head.

"Open your eyes, Dr. Slade," he teased.

She did, and foggy blue smacked him in the heart, causing his breath to stop in his throat. She was so damn beautiful but never more so than when she was flushed with pleasure, bleary-eyed from an intense orgasm.

It was his favorite look on her.

Carrick pushed her hair off her glistening forehead, his thumbs tracing the delicate arch of her brows, sweeping over those impossibly long eyelashes.

He could stare at her forever…

Uncomfortable with the thought, Carrick pushed his way inside her, sighing when he slid into warmth and wonderfulness.

This, he thought when he was deeply seated within her, this was something else he could do for the rest of his life.

Moving in her, hearing her sigh, then her moan, feeling her respond to him despite having multiple orgasms a minute before made him feel…yeah, invincible.

Powerful.

Yes, this was what he was damn good at.

This he could do…

Eight

After kissing Beth on the cheek, Sadie slid into her seat at the cozy bistro just doors down from Murphy International. Pulling her gloves off with her teeth, she shoved them into the pocket of the coat she'd draped over the back of her chair and picked up the laminated menu.

"What are we eating? I'm starving."

Making love with Carrick had, yet again, made her late and she'd skipped breakfast. She'd answered Beth's text to meet her for lunch with five happy faces, a dancing woman and a few thumbs-up.

Soup, Sadie decided. Chicken soup sounded perfect on a cold winter's day.

Sadie gave her order to the waitress, asked for some tea and looked at her friend's face. At some point she'd have to tell Beth that she was pregnant and it was a conversation she wasn't looking forward to. Beth was still concerned about Sadie's relationship with Carrick, and hearing that she was having his baby might make Beth's head explode.

Sadie loved Beth, she did, but her friend's protective streak was overblown and a trifle annoying.

But Sadie wouldn't spoil today's lunch by having another argument with Beth. If they stuck to discussing business, they'd be fine.

"Did you manage to set up that appointment for me at the Bethel Institute?" Sadie asked, smiling her thanks when the waitress placed her tea on the table in front of her.

"Yep," Beth said, casting an anxious look toward the door.

Sadie frowned, wondering why the usually efficient Beth was distracted.

"Anything else I should know about?" Sadie asked, her unease growing.

"I emailed you," Beth told her as she stood up and waved. Sadie, feeling eyes on her back and the hair rising on her arms, slowly turned around and saw Tamlyn, dressed in a black wool mini dress, black tights and knee-high boots walking across the coffee shop. A cashmere coat lay over her arm and her copper-colored hair glistened with raindrops.

Sadie turned her head and narrowed her eyes at Beth, looking defiant. "Why is Tamlyn joining us for lunch, Beth?" Sadie asked.

"We've all had lunch together on numerous occasions," Beth airily replied, but Sadie wasn't fooled. She recognized an intervention; she'd experienced one before.

"I'm not happy about this, Beth."

Beth didn't have time to answer as a wall of strong perfume hit them. Then slim arms clutched Sadie to Tamlyn's too-skinny frame and Sadie felt Tamlyn's lips on her right cheek, then her left.

Tamlyn eventually released Sadie and slid into the chair next to her sister, folded her hands on the table and looked at Sadie as if she were a fifteen-year-old who'd just been caught skipping school. If a single "tut" left her mouth, Sadie might lose it.

"Well, well, well."

Okay, it wasn't a tut but it was just as bad. Sadie shot Beth an annoyed glance before raising her eyebrows at Tamlyn. "Do you have a problem, Tamlyn?"

Tamlyn rotated the big diamond ring on her left finger and Sadie wondered if it was her engagement ring from Carrick and, if it was, why the hell was she still wearing it?

"Beth tells me that you and Carrick are seeing each other," Tamlyn stated, and Sadie leaned back, not liking the hellfire in the woman's eyes.

"Since we are both single and consenting adults, that has nothing to do with you," Sadie replied, keeping her voice even.

"And may I point out how deeply unprofessional you are both being?" Tamlyn asked, her voice sugary sweet.

Sadie's work hadn't been compromised; if anything, she was working harder than she normally did because of her relationship with Carrick.

Not that she'd explain that to Carrick's ex.

"You may not."

Tamlyn didn't even look remotely chastised. "I'm not sticking my nose into your business because it's fun, Sadie. I just don't want you to get hurt. Carrick is not a nice guy. You know this."

Actually, she didn't. Sadie now believed the exact opposite was true. "I don't feel comfortable discussing Carrick with you, Tamlyn."

"You were happy to discuss him before," Tamlyn pointed out.

She had her there.

"Rick was a horrible husband, Sadie."

She hated that Tamlyn called him Rick and she really, really, really wanted to wipe that patronizing smile off her face. Why had Sadie never noticed that Tamlyn's smile was hard, her eyes calculating?

She'd been such a sucker.

She'd wanted to believe Tamlyn, had needed to believe that Sadie wasn't the only one who'd thought she'd married one man only to get another.

She'd been so wrapped up in her own pain, in her own anger. Oh, she could justify her actions: her parents hadn't believed her, neither had her friends so she'd chosen to believe Tamlyn, knowing how difficult it was to see one version of a man and have the rest of the world seeing another.

But in this case, Tamlyn was wrong. And she was also malicious. Carrick wasn't the bad man she'd portrayed; he wasn't the abusive spouse she'd claimed. Tamlyn was distorting the facts to suit her own agenda.

Sadie knew Carrick; her heart recognized him. She might even…oh, dear…*love* Carrick. But more important, she saw him clearly. He wasn't an easy man and certainly didn't wear his heart on his sleeve.

But underneath the reticence was a strong, occasionally tender heart, and he was a man who danced to his own song, who didn't need the approval of others.

He was strong but kind.

Beth touched Sadie's hand with the tips of her fingers. "We're just trying to protect you, Sadie. You made a really bad decision before and we don't want to see you make another one."

Sadie pulled her hand away and shook her head, tired of Beth reminding her not to trust her own judgment.

Sadie picked up her spoon and drew patterns on the linen tablecloth. Given the information she'd had at the time—Dennis was charming, attentive, sweet and seemed to be totally in love with her—had she made the wrong decision? He was everything she, and every other woman she knew, wanted in a man. So had she really made such a bad decision? How was she supposed to know Dennis would turn into a monster?

She couldn't, unfortunately, look beneath the surface of a person's psyche and see the black mess below. That wasn't a superpower she possessed.

She'd made the correct decision based on all the information she had. She hadn't done anything wrong...

Dennis, that superb conman, was at fault, not her.

Maybe there wasn't anything wrong with her judgment. And maybe, just maybe, she should start to trust herself again.

Sadie leaned back and stared out the window of the upmarket bistro, not seeing the wet and dismal day beyond the cold pane. Sadie could feel something uncurling inside her soul, felt her heart starting to stretch.

It felt good, dammit.

More than good, it felt amazing.

And she wouldn't allow the Sturgis sisters to poison it. Being around them, listening to them, was toxic and she was done. Sadie looked at Tamlyn, taking in her perfect makeup and artfully arranged hair.

Pretty but poisonous.

And Beth's loyalty would always be to her sister. Sadie understood it, but she needed to break the cycle.

Enough. She was done.

Sadie heard the ringing of her phone from her bag and pounced on the device, thankful for the distraction. Seeing Carrick's name on her screen had her heart jumping and her lips curving. He made her heart smile. How could that be a bad thing?

"Hey, Carrick." She emphasized his full name and saw Tamlyn's eyebrows pull together.

"You left early this morning. Why didn't you wake me?" Carrick's deep voice washed over her. Sadie smiled and for the first time since she sat down, she felt at ease. Carrick made her feel like that; Tamlyn and Beth did not.

Sadie saw the look the sisters exchanged and ignored them, choosing to focus on the man on the other side of her call. "I needed to work and I'm leaving for the airport soon."

"Remind me where you are going and when you'll be back?"

"Depending on what information I find at the Virginia Museum of History and Culture, I'll be back the day after tomorrow."

Carrick didn't immediately reply and when the silence lengthened, Sadie fought the urge to break it.

"I'm going to miss you."

So good things did come to those who waited.

His voice was sandpaper rough, coated with emotion and his few words, quietly uttered, were the equivalent of him handing her the moon. Conscious of her audience, Sadie softly told him that she'd miss him, too.

Carrick cleared his throat. "Oh, by the way, I think you left some pills on the bathroom counter."

Sadie frowned. "I don't think I did. I scooped up all my toiletries when I left."

"Well, I'm holding a bottle of vitamins for pregnant women and another container labeled as folic acid."

Her pregnancy vitamins. Dammit. She'd forgotten all about them. "Ah, dammit."

"What's folic acid?"

Happy to be talking to him, and still hearing the

emotion in his voice, Sadie placed her elbow on the table and rested her cheek in her hand, allowing her hair to be a barrier between her and the outside world.

Sadie smiled at his pronunciation of the vitamin. But she couldn't explain; Beth and Tamlyn were listening to her side of the conversation. "Suffice to say that its necessary for the proper development of the process."

"Ah. Then you shouldn't miss a dose. Where are you? I'll bring them to you right now."

Sadie grinned at the concern in his voice. "That's really not necessary. I can easily pick up more." She glanced at her watch. "And I have to leave in the next ten minutes if I'm going to make my flight."

"Don't rush. Stress is bad for the baby. And for you."

His concern, and his tenderness, melted her from the inside out. "I'm fine, really."

"Don't push yourself too hard. Try and get some rest on the plane."

Touched, Sadie didn't point out that it was a ninety-minute flight from Boston to Richmond. "I'll keep in touch."

"I'm about to go into a series of meetings so I'll be going dark for pretty much the rest of the day. But be safe, okay?"

"Will do."

"Hurry home, sweetheart."

Sadie heard his call disconnect and closed her eyes, wanting to hold on to the dizzy-making, soul-jumping feeling. This was what falling in love felt

like, this deep-in-her-heart feeling of completeness.
Suddenly, the impossible—a future together, being
together as they raised their child, living and loving
and fighting and touching—seemed possible.

It was a heady feeling...

"You're crazy about him." Tamlyn's words were
coated with accusation.

Yep, she was.

"Are you insane?" Beth's question sounded a tad
screechy. "Has nothing we told you about him pen-
etrated your stubborn head?"

Without Beth's trust and support, Sadie didn't
know how they could continue to be friends. As for
working together... Beth was a great virtual assistant
but she was also privy to all Sadie's personal information. If she couldn't trust Beth on a personal level,
could she trust her with business details?

Sadie shook her head. "Beth, your determination
to interfere in something that has nothing to do with
you is hurting our friendship and our working relationship. It needs to stop. Right now."

"Don't talk to her like that, Sadie. She's just trying
to help you. Carrick is bad news. What will it take
for you to believe that?"

Beth sent Tamlyn a panicked look, obviously
caught in the middle. Sadie wasn't going to ask her
to choose between her and her sister—she'd probably
lose if she did—but she wouldn't tolerate them bad-
mouthing Carrick.

But neither did she need to give Tamlyn any information to spread around.

"I like Carrick…" Jeez, she could practically feel her nose growing longer with that lie. "I genuinely think he's a nice guy. We are friends. That's all that's between us."

Yep, her nose was definitely an inch longer.

But it wasn't a complete lie; they *were* friends. She was in love with him, he wasn't in love with her and friends-sharing-sex was probably all they'd ever be.

Sadie sent Tamlyn a hard look. "And I genuinely believe you've badly maligned him, possibly because he had the balls to get out of a toxic marriage. But apart from being my client, he's also my friend and I refuse to listen to anything else you have to say about him."

"But…"

Sadie held up her hand to stop Tamlyn from speaking. "No, I'm done listening to you. And if there's a whiff of speculation in the press about us, about Carrick, I'm coming after you, Tamlyn." Sadie turned her determined glance onto Beth. "And I do not want to hear another negative word from you about Carrick ever again, Beth. Are we clear?"

Beth nodded, her expression sulky.

She wasn't getting off that easy. "I need to hear you say the words, Elizabeth."

Yeah, she was using full names to get her point across.

"Yes, okay…jeez!"

Sadie wanted to call her out on her tone and her massive eye roll, but this wasn't the place and she was out of time. Standing up, she picked up her tote bag and put it over her shoulder.

Feeling exhausted, Sadie rested her hand on the handle of her overnight case and tapped the stack of books she left on the table.

"Beth, I've sent you a couple of emails. Please deal with those. And please contact the property management company in Paris and tell them that I am not renewing my lease on the apartment in Montparnasse."

She saw the questions and concern on Beth's face and shook her head. It would be a while, if ever, before she felt comfortable sharing her thoughts and feelings with Beth again. "And please return these books to Finn Murphy when you next head that way. If he's not available you can leave them with his PA, Cole."

Beth nodded. "Okay."

Ignoring Tamlyn, Sadie told Beth she'd be in touch and walked away, pulling her suitcase behind her. Tamlyn was out of her life, and Sadie's relationship with Beth was forever changed.

All because Sadie chose to believe her intuition about Carrick.

Man, she hoped she'd made the right call.

Joa followed Keely into the Irish pub and, over her shoulder, saw Tanna waving at them across the room. Joa smiled at her enthusiasm and then noticed the Brogan twins sitting on the bar stools on either side of her. Their oldest friend Darby stood next to Jules and they all watched Joa and Keely's progress across the room.

The whole gang was here.

Yay.

Joa pulled a smile onto her face and tried to look enthusiastic. Girls' nights out weren't her thing, but Keely, as bossy as hell, had nagged her into joining this one, telling Joa that she needed an uncomplicated evening with uncomplicated people.

The Brogan twins and Keely were Boston royalty and Darby was the daughter of a well-known judge. They were smart, sophisticated and successful...

Joa was...not.

She fought the urge to bolt and when Keely's hand encircled her wrist, she knew her friend was holding her in place. "You are not that fourteen-year-old runaway anymore, Joa Jones," Keely hissed.

Joa tossed her a sour look. "We have nothing in common, Keely."

"Rubbish. They are nice people and when you forget about that chip on your shoulder, you are, too. Now, smile, dammit!"

Joa tried to tug her wrist from Keely's iron-clad grip, but Keely was stronger than any restraint. Knowing that she was risking a scene, Joa followed Keely to her friends and hung back when they all exchanged what seemed to be genuine hugs.

Joa, not being the touchy-feely type, kept herself out of hugging distance.

Tanna smiled at her and asked what she wanted to drink. When they all placed their orders, Keely turned her attention back to Joa. "What's the situation with you and Ronan? Are you going to help him out or not?"

This again? Lord, she'd forgotten how pushy Keely could be. What she hadn't forgotten was Ronan Murphy standing in his kitchen, looking messy and fierce and frustrated and so very sexy, muscles rippling under his tanned skin. Those memories ambushed her constantly.

She thought about him far more than she should...

Keely didn't wait for her to answer. "Poor Ronan is pulling his hair out trying to work and look after them."

Why was that her problem? There were agencies and nannies in Boston—surely finding one wasn't the impossibility Keely made it out to be?

Before she could respond, Tanna, Ronan's petite sister, jumped into the conversation. "Listen, I've heard some stories about my brothers when they were young that would curl your toes. I suspect Ro is raising himself. Times two."

Joa accepted her glass of wine, smiling at Tanna's fond but frank assessment of her brother. She could easily imagine Ronan raising hell.

Joa looked around and didn't see Sadie, the one person she actually knew. "Sadie isn't here?"

Keely shook her head. "She's gone to Virginia to do some research on our Homer."

"Our *possible* Homer," Joa corrected her. There was no point in getting their hopes up.

Keely ignored her and raised her eyebrows at Tanna. "How do you feel about becoming an aunt again?"

Tanna smiled. "I'm over the moon. I just hope this one is a girl. I don't know if this family can cope with more boys."

Keely laughed. "But can you imagine Carrick with a daughter? He was super-protective of you growing up. Can you imagine how overprotective he will be of his daughter?"

Tanna pulled a face. "Sadie will keep him in line. I hope."

Darby sucked on her straw, her attention captured by a commotion at the door. "Well, wow."

They all turned around to look. Four impossibly good-looking guys stood by the entrance shedding their coats.

"Darby Brogan-Huntley, you are so married!" Tanna said, laughter in her voice.

Ignoring the thought that none of those men were as sexy as Ronan, Joa jumped into the conversation. "But I'm not. In fact, I'm very, very single. Who are they?"

Keely slapped her arms across her chest and glared at the foursome who were heading toward the pool room to the left of the bar. "Those are the Seymour brothers. The one on the far left is the executor of our estate, Joa, Wilfred 'Dare' Seymour. How can you not know that?"

Well, easily, since she'd only very briefly met the man, and, at the time, she'd been coping with soul sucking grief over Isabel's death. Since returning home she'd heard a litany of complaints about Dare Seymour but Keely had never once mentioned that he was tall, dark and sinfully sexy.

Purely to wind Keely up, Joa placed her tongue in her cheek. "He's really hot. I think I need to be formally introduced to him."

"Do it and die," Keely seethed.

When none of them could contain their laughter,

Keely tossed her hair and defiantly downed her glass of wine. "This is a girls' night out and we're not going to hit on, ogle or drool over any men."

Aw, but wasn't that one of the joys of a girls' night out? At least for single women?

Oh, well, it didn't matter since none of the Seymour clan could hold a candle to the current star of her sexual fantasies.

In Richmond, Sadie sat cross-legged on the bed in her very boring hotel room and squinted at the appalling picture on the wall opposite her. Call her spoiled but she'd spent a lot of time in Carrick's house lately and his art collection was fantastic. Looking at generic, boring images as she went to bed was a hell of a crash back to earth. And reality.

She loved Carrick's house, loved the big rooms and the molded ceilings and original black-and-white-tiled floors. Okay, it was a little tired decor-wise, but nothing a paint job, new drapes and a few scatter cushions couldn't sort out.

When the baby came, they'd have to remove the precious and breakable items from the desks and tables, and put childproof locks on the cupboards and a security gate at the top of the stairs…

Oh, God, she was acting like she was going to live there, like she had a say in how to decorate and childproof his house.

She didn't…

She was just the mother of his child, and his current lover.

And if she kept hoping and dreaming and planning, she would be setting herself up for a hell of a fall. It would be a long, painful plummet back to earth. *Be sensible, Slade. Keep your expectations reality-based.* And she should be thinking about where she wanted to live as she no longer had an apartment in Paris to run back to. Should she rent something close to Carrick's house or should she buy a house? Could she even afford to buy anything in Carrick's expensive area? Leaning forward, Sadie tapped her laptop keyboard and quickly entered a search for houses into her browser.

Rolling through the options for sale, she grimaced at the prices of Beacon Hill properties.

Her business was doing well, but not *that* well.

She'd probably have to rent. Or look for a house in a less salubrious part of Boston. But one that had good schools.

Or would Carrick expect their child to attend the same expensive schools he did? She didn't know how she felt about private school education; she'd attended public schools and she'd turned out okay...

They had so much to talk about. Discipline, schooling, manners, visitation rights...

Feeling a little overwhelmed, Sadie fell backward, her head hitting the pillow. At some point they'd have to make decisions. They couldn't keep operating in a sexual haze forever.

She wanted to, but it wasn't practical...

Her phone buzzed and Sadie patted the bed next to her, looking for the device. Picking it up, she held it close and squinted at the screen.

Where are you? What are you doing?

Her lips curved upward and her heart bounced off her chest. Carrick.

In my hotel room. She hesitated, wondering if she was brave enough to tell him how she was feeling. I'm looking at an awful painting and missing...

She deliberately stopped there, wanting to tease.

Missing what?

She laughed out loud while she typed. Your art. Sadie waited for a few beats before typing again.

And you.

Good answer. What are you wearing?

Sadie looked down at her yoga pants and baggy sweatshirt and knew that she had to lie.

Nothing.

Mmm. Have you ordered something to eat?

Sadie wrinkled her nose. She'd expected him to reply with some sexy comment, not to nag her about eating.

I'm waiting for room service. They should be here any second.

She saw that Carrick had read her message and sighed when she heard the sharp rap on her door. Climbing off the bed, she typed another message to Carrick.

Stop nagging. My food has arrived.

Not checking the peephole, she wrenched the door open, her eyes on her phone, waiting for Carrick's reply. When she didn't hear the rumble of a food cart, she looked up and her heart nearly exploded when she saw him standing in her doorway, a scowl on his masculine face.

Sadie squealed, launched herself at him and he caught her as she jumped into his arms, her legs wrapping around his waist.

Sadie rained kisses on his face, so damn happy to see him. "Yay, you're here," she said in between kisses. "Why are you here?"

Carrick gently covered her face with his big hand to stop her kisses. "I was missing you and I haven't used my plane in a while."

Sadie leaned back to look into his amused face. "You have a plane?"

"Mmm."

Her eyes danced with mischief. "Hassan has a Gulfstream. How big is yours?"

"I'm not going to get into a plane-measuring contest with your Arab prince, Slade," Carrick told her. He carried her farther into the room and kicked the door shut. "But I do have a couple of questions for you, Doctor."

Sadie ran her fingers over his cheek, along his jaw. "Can they wait?"

"No. Why didn't you check the peephole before you opened the door? I could've been any old serial killer."

Sadie leaned forward and kissed the side of his mouth, inhaling his gorgeous cologne. "God, I love the way you smell," she murmured.

Carrick squeezed her butt. "And that leads me to my second question...why did you lie to me?"

Sadie pulled back and frowned at him. "What are you talking about?"

"You said you were naked." He held her with one arm and tugged at the round neck of her sweatshirt. "Clearly you are not."

Ah. "Well, that can be easily remedied."

"I was hoping you'd say that," Carrick said, gently lowering her to the bed. He stood up and glanced across the room. "And, God, yes, that painting is damn ugly." He looked down at her, his smile charmingly crooked. "But you sure as hell aren't."

Nine

Carrick had plans to leave work early today since Sadie was flying in from Richmond—her return delayed by two long days—and they'd agreed to dinner at his place. He'd already had Marsha arrange for delivery of oysters, champagne and beef Wellington from Geraint's, an exclusive caterer who provided meals to crazies like him who needed special food at the last minute.

He planned on opening a bottle of champagne Krug Clos d'Ambonnay 1995, despite the fact that Sadie wouldn't enjoy more than a sip of the four-thousand-dollar bottle. He'd been keeping the bottle for a special occasion but Sadie was, in herself, a special occasion.

And possibly the best thing that happened to him in, well, forever.

And he'd missed her, probably more than he should. He'd considered making another trip to Richmond to see her, but he got bogged down at work and while his partners might overlook one quick, non-work-related trip in the jet, they might object to a second one in less than a week.

But damn, he'd been tempted to personally cover the costs and just go.

Because, despite only knowing each other for a brief period, he'd missed waking up to her, rolling over and pulling her body into his and dropping back off to sleep. Or rolling over and not dropping back to sleep.

Carrick shut down his laptop and closed the lid. Something had changed between him and Sadie; something had fundamentally shifted and he wanted it defined, explained, to pull whatever they were feeling into the light. This wasn't love, not yet, but it was close. And he wanted to know if he was the only one along for the ride.

Carrick stood and placed his hand on the back of his chair and looked out his window, smiling at the weak sunlight trying to penetrate the low clouds. The sky reminded him of John La Farge's *Snow Storm*… hell, the woman even had him relating everything he saw back to art.

Carrick leaned his shoulder into the glass and stared down, his thoughts a million miles away. He was crazy about Sadie; he had been since the first time she walked into his office in that Bohemian dress and boots. She challenged him, intrigued and fascinated him and, yes, he was completely obsessed with her body...

And that was even before he threw in the added complication of her carrying his child...

Was he falling for her too fast? Was this another woman who was going to break his heart? Few knew him well enough to know that under his corporate persona was a bit of a romantic—a man who'd always wanted a family, a wife, someone he could call his own.

He'd thought he'd missed his chance when he divorced Tamlyn, mostly because he refused to put himself in the position of allowing another woman to hurt him. He'd tried to keep his defenses up with Sadie but she'd snuck her way into his life, filling up those cold and empty spaces in his heart and life with her sharp mind and vivacious personality.

Carrick knew Sadie saw him clearly, that she was no longer influenced by the stories she'd heard via Tamlyn and Beth. She knew him...he could see it in her eyes, feel it in her touch, in the way she handed herself over to him, trusting him to not only pleasure her, but to also keep her safe and treat her well. He no longer heard doubt in her voice and hadn't seen that speculative look in her eyes for weeks.

It had taken a little time, but he was convinced that Sadie, with no explanation from him, now saw him for the man he was.

And that man was crazy about her.

And, God, he hoped she was feeling the same.

Either way, he needed to know. If they were both slipping into something deeper, more meaningful, then they could plan to raise their child together, two parents in one house and hopefully, in time, his ring on her finger.

But if he was the only one who was feeling a little mushy, he needed to find out now so he could shut down any growing feelings. And he would shut them down, without her suspecting a damn thing. He'd never beg her to love him.

Love, not freely given, wasn't worth a damn.

But they were at a crossroads, and one of them had to take the first step, to open the dialogue. And, yeah, if a super-expensive bottle of Krug made that conversation easier, he wasn't going to think about the four-thousand-dollar price tag.

Sadie was worth it.

Sadie was worth…

Close to everything.

Carrick heard the brief knock on his door and looked around to see his younger brother Finn in the open doorway, his dark blond hair as shaggy as always. Finn was dressed in his usual uniform of designer jeans and a black button-down shirt, sleeves rolled up above his wrists.

Unlike Carrick and Ronan, who were in the public eye, Finn spent most of his time in the basement of the building, which he'd converted into an office-cum-library-cum-lab. His researchers shared an open-plan office on the next floor up, but the basement was

Finn's domain and they rarely disturbed him when he was holed up in his inner sanctum. Finn needed quiet and solitude to work effectively and since he was a genius at what he did—research and provenance and detecting—Carrick and Ronan left him alone.

Finn came up for air when he wanted to, and it was always a pleasure to spend time with his youngest brother.

Except for today, when he'd really wanted to get home early.

But because he was the CEO and Finn's older brother, he waved Finn in. Finn immediately headed for the hidden bar fridge and pulled from it two bottles of water. He tossed one at Carrick, who snapped his hand around the bottle. He didn't want water; he wanted Sadie and that champagne.

And that conversation.

Patience, Carrick. You have time...

"What's up?"

Finn dropped his lanky body into one of his visitor's chairs and gave a detailed but succinct progress report on where they stood on cataloging Isabel's collection. Interesting, but a topic that could've waited until tomorrow.

"We are down to the last floor of Mounton House, which was where the servants lived."

Carrick resisted the urge to look at his watch and forced the question out. "And the attic?"

"We still need to get into the attic, but I don't hold much hope of finding anything of value up there. I think we've got everything of value already."

"But you're going to check, right?"

Finn gave him a look. "Of course I am."

Okay, good. Carrick sent a longing look at his open door.

Finn rested his ankle on his opposite knee and rested his bottle on his thigh. "Isabel was the proud owner of a Manet, a Rothko and many Georgia O'Keeffes. There are some negatives by Ansel Adams and a rare jade bird from the Shang dynasty."

Carrick could never remember the Chinese dynasties. "Which was when?"

"We estimate it to be from fifteen hundred years before Christ."

Carrick whistled. Even in his business that was old.

"I've sent you an updated list of what we are selling," Finn told him.

Carrick nodded his thanks and deliberately looked at his watch, knowing that Finn would take the hint. When Finn didn't move, Carrick frowned. "Anything else, Finn? I'm trying to get out of here."

"Are you seeing Sadie tonight?" Finn looked uncomfortable, and Carrick felt his heart thud, and not in a good way. His youngest brother was intensely private, a bit of a loner, and he hated people prying into his life. As a result, he never ever interfered in anyone else's, and Carrick could count the times on one hand that Finn poked his nose where it didn't belong.

"I am," Carrick said.

Finn nodded, still looking unsure, another hint that he wasn't happy with the direction of the conversation. "Okay. How goes the search for provenance on the potential Homer?"

"Sadie is on her way back from Richmond, and I'm hoping she has news." Carrick rested his forearms on the back of his office chair and gave his brother a hard look. "Stop beating around the bush and ask me what you really want to ask me, Finn."

"I was just wondering how you and Sadie are going to make it work, raising a child together when you are living on two different continents."

Carrick frowned at him, not understanding his comment. "I'm not sure what you are getting at. While Sadie and I haven't nailed down the details of how we are going to raise our kid, I did understand that we would be doing it together."

"In Boston?"

"That's where we live, Finn."

"But she's going back to Paris."

Carrick swallowed the urge to laugh. He grinned and shook his head. "Nope, she has an apartment in Montparnasse but she's relocating to Boston."

Finn leaned forward, his expression radiating concern. "Did she tell you that or did you just assume that?"

He'd assumed that.

Carrick felt a hard, cold ball settle in his stomach. He jammed his hands into the pockets of his pants so Finn wouldn't see them shaking. "Again, it's not like you to beat around the bush, Finn."

Finn rubbed the back of his neck, and Carrick saw that his discomfort was sky-high. "I feel like I am snitching, but the conversation took place in front of me. Nobody was trying to hide anything. But maybe I should go…it has nothing to do with me."

God help him. "Spit it out, Finn."

"Beth, your ex-sister-in—"

For the love of everything holy… "I know who Beth is, Finn."

Finn's uneasiness ratcheted up. "She dropped off some books I loaned Sadie and she was just about to leave when she took a call. She was in my office, standing on the other side of my desk so I couldn't help listening in on her conversation. What she didn't realize is that I am fluent in French."

He was also fluent in German, Spanish and could converse in Mandarin and read Japanese. Finn had a gift for languages… And a gift for math, science and any type of learning and literature. Carrick just wished he didn't love adrenaline as much as he loved books. He could do without knowing that his brother threw himself off buildings with just a parachute or dashed down steep passes and trails on a mountain bike.

You're avoiding the issue, Murphy, trying to distract yourself.

Finn had stopped talking and Carrick knew he wouldn't continue if Carrick didn't encourage him to do so. He could just walk out of here, right now, and everything would be as it was before Finn opened his mouth.

But he knew himself well; not knowing would drive him nuts.

"Just tell me, goddammit."

"Sadie is going back to France. I know how important it is to you to be a part of your child's life, be a dad. How are you going to see your kid if she's living in Paris?"

Carrick felt the punch to his heart, the fist squeezing his stomach. Finn had to be wrong, he told himself. "Why would you think she's going back to Paris?"

Finn winced, his eyes sympathetic. "Why else would she be renewing the lease on her apartment in Montparnasse? Because Beth was talking to her landlord, and she asked him to courier her a new lease for signature."

Carrick dug his fingers into his chair and stared at his brother, wanting him to pull his words back, to say he was joking, pulling a prank. When Finn just held his gaze, his eyes not showing a hint of amusement, Carrick accepted that his brother wasn't yanking his chain.

Sadie was intending to go back to France when her contract with Murphy's was over. Since she hadn't spoken to him about living in France, nor even hinted at her plans, he was obviously not a factor in her decision.

Hurt, hot and sour, rolled over him.

What a surprise, he'd done it again. He'd fallen first, he'd fallen harder and, yet again, fallen for the wrong person. And he was obviously far closer to falling in love than he thought because he ached, dammit. Icy fingers clutched his heart and his stomach twisted itself into a knot.

When would he ever learn?

Sadie skipped up the steps to Carrick's Beacon Hill house, her heart in her throat and bats in her stomach. She'd missed Carrick so much and the tender, funny messages they'd exchanged over the past few days—and the fact that he'd commandeered the company plane to spend the night with her—gave her hope that they'd turned a corner, that something was growing between them that was precious and special and...

Right.

Like Tab A that was designed to slip into Slot B, they fit.

Carrick would be an amazing partner, an incredible significant other and a brilliant father. As she'd come to learn, he was a good man. He worked hard, took care of his family, treated his staff with respect and, best of all, he was, she was sure, a little crazy about her.

Maybe also a little in love with her. Or was she jumping the gun? No, she'd seen the way he looked at her, with lust and amusement and tenderness and buckets of hope, and she wasn't imagining a damn thing.

Sadie touched her belly, cradling her tummy, and closed her eyes to enjoy the surge of emotion coursing through her. Her baby was healthy, she was in love and she was pretty confident her love would be returned. Maybe not today but sometime...

Sometime soon...

Sadie lifted her hand to ring the doorbell and hesitated, remembering that just a few months before, love had been a concept she no longer believed in. She'd genuinely believed she would never be happy and hopeful again.

How silly she'd been...and, yeah, she owed Carrick for opening her up to love again. And maybe she'd been meant to marry Dennis, to experience the worst of love before she could appreciate what a good man looked like, how he acted.

Maybe she'd needed to howl and curse and feel like crap so that when the right man arrived, she could say, "Yes, this is right. This is who I've been waiting for."

Maybe she'd needed to experience the bad so she could recognize the exceptional.

Because Carrick was exceptional, in and out of bed.

And talking about bed, she really hoped he liked the sexy lingerie she'd picked up in Richmond, a barely there number that enhanced rather than concealed, that tempted and tantalized. She was wearing jeans and an aqua cashmere thigh-length sweater, nice enough, but not terribly sexy so her lingerie should be a pleasant shock.

Although she doubted she'd keep it on for long.

Sadie grinned, the door opened and there he was...

Sadie, unable to help herself, flung herself into his arms, winding her arms around his neck and lifting her face for a kiss. But instead of ducking his head, Carrick placed his hands on her hips and lifted her off him to place her feet on the ground.

Sadie brushed her hair out of her eyes, looked up into his face and her smile faded. Something was wrong, she just knew it.

Sadie felt both boiling hot and icy cold, breathless and heartsore. Pain rolled through her body. She didn't understand why, but she did know that her and Carrick's relationship had taken a one-eighty and flipped upside down.

It was over. She knew that without him having to say one word.

But what could possibly have happened between now and his last text message at lunchtime? The words were burned into her brain she'd read it so often:

Hey, sweetheart, I'm going into a series of meetings this afternoon so might not respond immediately if you send me a message. But I'm thinking of you and can't wait to see you later. Get some sleep on the plane. You're going to need it because I intend keeping you awake for most of the night.

Sadie pulled a tremulous smile onto her face, hoping and praying she was wrong. She *had* to be wrong. "Hi."

"Sadie." Carrick shoved his hands into the pockets of his suit pants, and Sadie noted that he still wore his suit jacket and his tie was still perfectly knotted.

This was Carrick, the hard-assed CEO, not Carrick, her lover. "Everything okay?"

She knew it wasn't, but she wasn't going to go with her first impulse—to drop to her knees, wind her arms around his legs and beg him to tell him what she'd done wrong.

Because she hadn't done anything wrong. She hadn't had time to mess up.

"No."

Sadie forced the words through her numb lips. "A little more information please."

Carrick took his time answering her. "I think we are making a huge mistake continuing to sleep together. We're not going to be a happy family. We're not going to live together and raise our child together."

Wow.

Sadie felt the punch of his words and she took a step back, trying to get away from the impact. His expression was implacable, but his eyes burned with fury. His hands, still in his pockets, were bunched into fists, and tension made the cords in his neck more prominent. Carrick was furious. Memories of another man's face, and his vicious expression, tumbled over her. Falling back into that memory, she took another step back, needing to put space between her and the much bigger Carrick.

Which was ridiculous; this was Carrick, not Dennis. Carrick, no matter how angry he was, wouldn't hurt her...knowing she was painting him by that other brush, she lowered her shoulders and told herself that she had nothing to fear—

"Jesus, you think I might hurt you?" Carrick roared.

Sadie winced. Of course, Carrick would pick up on her movements. He was an observant guy at the best of times and he paid her a lot of attention. "No—"

"I am not your ex!"

His words bounced off the walls of the hallway and echoed through the large house. Sadie lifted her hands, desperately looking for the right words. "I know you aren't—"

"You haven't changed your mind about me at all, have you?" Carrick demanded. It wasn't a shout, but it wasn't far off, either. Sadie stood up straighter and took a step closer, needing to show him that she wasn't scared of him. She knew that he would never, ever hurt her physically.

Though he was doing a damn fine job of hurting her emotionally.

"Carrick, I—"

"You're still judging me by what you heard from my ex-wife! And if that's the case, why are you sleeping with me? What's your angle?"

Sadie felt his verbal bullets piercing her heart. How had something so beautiful turned so ugly? What was happening here?

"I don't have an angle! And I'm sleeping with you because I'm crazy about you. I can't stop thinking about you. Hell, I think I'm in love with you!" Sadie shouted back. Okay, that was not the way she'd wanted to tell him that she loved him. She'd wanted it to be a tender moment, emotional, hot and sweet. A memory she'd carry with her for the rest of her life.

Well, she'd definitely remember this!

"How dare you tell me that you feel like that when I know you have no intention of sticking around, when you plan on taking my child away from me? I'm not going to let that happen, Sadie. I've lost too many people in my life for that to happen."

"What the hell are you talking about?" Sadie demanded. He wasn't making any sense!

Carrick narrowed his eyes at her. "You're going back to Paris. You're renewing the lease on your apartment."

"Why on earth would you think that?"

Carrick pulled his hands from his pockets and slapped them across his chest. Sadie saw the misery underneath the hurt and she fought the urge to throw herself into his arms, to soothe away his pain. But she was in pain, too, and she needed to take care of herself first.

"Beth dropped off some books with Finn and he overheard her talking to your landlord, making arrangements to renew your lease on your apartment. Why would you do that unless you were planning to run away? And why play games with me? Are you trying to get back at me for what your ex did to you? Or do you secretly believe Tamlyn and you want to punish me on her behalf?"

Wow. And she thought her marriage had messed her up? Carrick had her beat.

"I'm not going back to Paris. I'm not playing games. I don't believe Tamlyn. Please believe *me*."

She heard her pleading tone, but she didn't care.

She needed to get through to him. She couldn't let him toss her—*them*—away.

But the fury in his eyes didn't diminish and Sadie knew she'd lost. Carrick had found something to drive a wedge between them, and because he was terrified of getting hurt again, he was using it to split them apart. This was the first hurdle in their relationship and he hadn't even tried to clear it. He'd just folded, choosing to believe the worst about her without getting her side of the story.

She didn't know if she could fight his distrust; she didn't know if she wanted to. She'd lived a life with a man where every day was a battle, where trust was a commodity he played with, that was dangled and removed, offered and rejected.

She wasn't going to play that game. She'd rather walk away right now than subject herself to that again.

Sadie reached down and picked up her bag that had fallen to the floor. She hoisted it over her shoulder and stared at her feet, trying to get her brain to form the necessary words. Or, better yet, she could just leave…

But she'd done that with Dennis. She'd never stood up for herself; she'd been too scared. He'd bullied her into silence. She refused to be silent again.

"Can I talk?" she asked Carrick.

He nodded.

"Without interruption?" Sadie pressed the point.

He nodded, quickly and sharply.

"Thank you." She had to remain calm; one of them ·should. And in her experience, calm words quietly stated had more impact than shouted words and turbulent emotion. Sadie gripped the handle of her bag and started to speak.

"You have a whole lot of nerve, Carrick Murphy. You wanted me to make up my own mind about you, without one single explanation about how and why your marriage ended. And that, by the way, is why I am with you, why I am 'playing' this game." She made air quotes with her fingers.

"Because I trust you. Correction, I did trust you. I trusted you to treat me well. But you won't trust me. I told you that we'd raise this child together, and while we haven't had many discussions about the mechanics of that arrangement, I thought it was a solid understanding between us."

She thought about the searches she'd done on houses, about the emails she'd sent to real estate agents the day before yesterday. "Up until fifteen minutes ago, I was rearranging my life so you could be a part of my and the baby's lives."

Sadie shook her fingers, trying not to let panic overwhelm her. "I could've just told you that I am having your child and that I'm going back to France to raise it and you can see him or her whenever you fly over. I didn't do that. I had plans to move back to Boston so our child could spend more time with his or her father."

Man, she felt gutted, stripped of everything that made her Sadie. But she had to get this out, no matter how hard it became. "I wanted to live in Boston because I also couldn't imagine living a life not being close to you, seeing you often, hopefully turning this burning attraction we have into a lifelong love affair."

Carrick opened his mouth to speak, but Sadie cut him off. He'd stated his case; it was her turn now.

"I'm not done. You wanted to mistrust me, Carrick, and you took the first opportunity to do that. I can't live like that, not again. I was at the mercy of a man who I constantly begged to trust me, to trust us, but he played games with me. And you accusing me of playing games, well, that hurts. And you know what? I'd rather not play at all."

Sadie hitched up the strap of her bag and, with her heart breaking, she spun around and headed for the front door.

She wouldn't stumble; she wouldn't cry. She would walk out of his house and his life with her head held high. She'd shed too many tears over stupid men and she wouldn't do it again. They weren't worth it.

When she hit the sidewalk, she heard his front door closing and it felt like the oversize exclamation mark at the end of their horrid conversation. Sadie, standing in the frigid wind, felt her eyes sting and her throat close.

It was only the cold that had her eyes watering, the icy wind stealing her breath. That was what she told herself. But then hot tears rolled down her cheeks and she knew she would cry over Carrick, probably for a long time.

She'd cry because he was a good man and she'd lost him. Not to cruelty or to manipulation, but to mistrust and fear.

And that was the saddest possible ending to their story.

Ten

"Sadie, I wasn't expecting you."

Even via the intercom, Sadie heard the note of displeasure in Beth's voice. Her friend had never been a fan of people dropping by unexpectedly.

But tough. Beth had messed with Sadie's life and she wasn't going to make a damn appointment to set Beth straight.

Sadie ran her hand over her head. She'd pulled her hair back into a ponytail, a style that made her look harder, older and tougher. She'd kept her makeup simple and this morning, after a sleepless night alternating between tears and anger, she'd slicked her lips in a shade of red lipstick that should be called don't-mess-with-me-today.

Sure, she was sad, hurt, but damn, she was also beyond pissed. With Beth, with Carrick, with her life.

Both Beth and Carrick, people she should be able to trust, had let her down. Sadie had never felt more adrift, lost. Was there ever going to be a time when she didn't feel so alone? Would she ever have someone to stand with her, her very own soft place to fall?

Right now she couldn't imagine that, couldn't envision a future with anyone but Carrick.

But a future with Carrick wasn't going to happen.

Her family had disappointed her by believing Dennis over her. Beth hadn't listened when Sadie told her to butt out of her life. And Carrick couldn't trust her.

Well, on the plus side she still had Hassan. God, why hadn't she listened to him?

"It's early, Sadie, and I'm not dressed," Beth said.

Weak excuse. "Beth, I've seen you in your pj's before. Open the damn door."

"Why are you here?"

"Oh, because you and I need to have a chat about how you deliberately gave Finn the impression that I was going back to France. You knew he would tell Carrick. You ambushed my relationship, Beth. Open the damn door."

Beth muttered a curse. "Give me ten minutes and I'll come down."

"I'll give you five minutes and if you don't let me in, I will lean on your doorbell until you do."

Beth didn't reply so Sadie presumed she'd agreed. If that door didn't click open in five, she would use the emergency key Beth had given to her years before, the key Beth had probably forgotten about.

Sadie hadn't and she was prepared to use it. But she still had five minutes to kill. Pulling out her phone, she stared down at the screen and dialed a number. She was in the mood to kick ass and it wasn't like she had anything to lose. The video call rang and then, for the first time in years, she saw her mom's face on the small screen.

"Sadie, are you okay?" To her credit, her mom's voice was threaded with a ribbon of fear. "What's wrong?"

"I'm fine, Mom. Is Dad there?" Sadie asked and then she saw her dad's face over her mom's shoulder, anxiety in his eyes, too.

"Hey, pumpkin."

Sadie narrowed her eyes at him. He'd lost the right to call her by her childhood nickname when he'd chosen Dennis over her. "I just called to tell you that I'm super-pissed at both of you. I am beyond hurt."

Two mouths dropped open in shock. Yep, bet they hadn't thought they would start off their Friday morning with a lecture from their estranged daughter.

Well, life, as she could tell them, didn't always go as planned.

"When my marriage fell apart, I needed you. I needed you to believe me when I told you how badly Dennis treated me. I needed your love and support. But you sided with him. You chose to believe a man you hardly knew instead of believing me."

"The things you said, they were, are, difficult to believe…"

Her mom's excuse made her temper bubble and pop. "Mom, I've never been a liar. And it's your job to stand by your kids. If my daughter ever comes to me and tells me that her husband is treating her like crap, I will take him on, no questions asked. My loyalty will be, forever and always, to my child. I will not disappoint her…or him. My child will always, always know that I have his back. You did not have my back. You still don't."

They were both making fish mouths, gulping in air. Sadie wasn't sure their silence was from shock or because she'd finally had the guts to confront them, to tell them how unhappy she was with their behavior. It didn't matter; she'd needed to clear the air, to express her disappointment. She didn't know if she'd have a relationship with them again, but that was okay. She'd needed to confront them, to stand up for herself.

Because if she couldn't stand up for herself, she'd never be able to stand up for her child.

"Wait…are you trying to tell us that you're pregnant?"

Her mom's words dragged Sadie back into the present. "Yes, I'm pregnant."

Her mom clapped her hands and her dad's eyes lit up. "That's so exciting!" her mom gushed. "Our first grandchild. Oh, baby, I'm beyond thrilled."

Sadie frowned down at the screen. "Wait, hold on…did you not hear a thing I said earlier?"

Her mom waved her words away. "That's in the past. This is a new chapter."

Really? Because it didn't feel that way to her. "No, you don't get to drop back into my life without an apology, pretending you didn't let me down, you didn't hurt me. If I hadn't called you, would you have called me?"

She didn't need an answer; she knew the truth. Sadie's fingertips drifted across her forehead. "Okay, so I'm going to hang up. This conversation is going nowhere, which I should've expected."

"Wait!"

Her dad's face filled the screen, his expression mortified. "Don't leave it like this, Sadie. What can we do to make this right?"

Sadie shrugged. "I don't know, Dad. I don't think it can be fixed."

"I want to try. I've missed you."

"Phones work both ways, Dad." But despite everything, she couldn't just walk away. These were her parents, and her child deserved to know the only set of grandparents he, or she, would have.

Sadie gripped the bridge of her nose. "I'm going through hell right now, so maybe you can call me in a couple of weeks and maybe we can meet. I'm not promising anything but…maybe."

"I'll call."

Maybe he would, maybe he wouldn't. But it was up to them now. Sadie said goodbye and disconnected the call. One argument down, another to go.

Courage, Slade. You can do this.

She was about to lean on Beth's doorbell again when the door opened and Beth stood there, her face anxious.

Before Sadie could utter a word, Beth started to speak. "I genuinely didn't know Finn spoke French. The landlord called me, not the other way around. It was a sheer fluke that I was in Finn's office when I took that call."

"I told you to cancel the lease," Sadie said, not sure whether to believe Beth or not.

"I know and I was going to do what you asked me but…" Beth's expression was pure misery and her words dried up. Her eyes filled with tears and her bottom lip trembled.

Sadie swallowed, reluctantly touched by her friend's obvious show of emotion, but also reminding herself that Beth's action had resulted in the rift between Sadie and Carrick.

But really, if it hadn't been Beth's phone call, it would've been something else. Carrick would've found another reason to push her away, to mistrust her. Her resentment toward her friend dropped a level and she tipped her head to the side.

"Explain."

"I wanted you to have a backup plan, in case things went wrong here in Boston. I know how much you love your apartment, how much you love Paris. That was where you fled to when things went south with Dennis. The city soothes you, you love the art, the vibe, the people. I asked your landlord to extend the lease by six months—after that I was going to either renew it or cancel it."

"I would've noticed a rental payment to the lease, Beth," Sadie said, exasperated.

"I was going to pay it. You wouldn't have known."

Sadie frowned, puzzled. "Beth, that apartment is expensive. Paris is expensive. You don't have that sort of money to pay for an apartment you'll never use."

Beth looked defiant. "I have enough savings to cover it."

Sadie ran her hands over her face, her anger draining away. Beth had been prepared to hand over her hard-earned savings just to make sure Sadie had a bolt hole, somewhere to run to where she felt safe. And if Finn hadn't overheard her plans, Sadie might never have known about Beth's generosity and sacrifice.

"I really hope you are going to be happy with Carrick, Sadie, and maybe Tam did exaggerate. She is a drama queen. But she's my sister," Beth said, her bottom lip quivering.

Sadie had wanted her family to trust her blindly, to believe everything she said about Dennis, but now she was angry at Beth for believing Tamlyn?

Sadie released a massive sigh and took her friend's cold hand. "Beth... Man, what a mess. I'm mad at you because your actions led to a confrontation with Carrick, but I just realized that if it didn't happen now, it would have happened later." She took a deep breath of cold air, felt the burn, but was grateful that the temperature banished the last of her anger toward her friend.

"We're not together anymore, but I'm not going back to Paris. My home is here now, in Boston. With or without Carrick, here is where I need to be."

Beth wiped away her tears. "You're not mad at me?"

Sadie managed a smile. "Slightly irritated, but that will pass." Her smile died when she realized it was time to come fully clean. "I don't want you to tell anyone, especially not Tamlyn, but I am pregnant. Carrick is the father and that's why I'm staying in Boston. I want my child to have time with their father and Carrick is a good man."

Beth stared, her eyes wide.

"You really believe that, don't you?" Instead of disparagement, Sadie heard wonder in Beth's voice.

"I don't believe it, Beth, I know it," Sadie replied, feeling like her heart was being ripped apart by the claws of a wolverine.

Beth squeezed her fingers. "I think it's time I started making up my own mind about your man, Sades."

Sadie managed a tremulous smile. "Unfortunately, he's not my man, Beth. Not anymore."

"Oh, honey, he really is." Beth reached out and Sadie felt arms around her, heard the clear but heartfelt apology Beth spoke in her ear. "Forgive me?"

Sadie, her throat clogged with tears, just nodded. Beth tugged her into the hallway and Sadie blinked to clear her vision. When she looked at Beth, her eyes were wet.

"So does this mean I'm not fired?" Beth asked, keeping their hands linked.

Sadie managed a quick, small smile. "Well, not today."

I don't have an angle! And I'm sleeping with you because I'm crazy about you. I can't stop thinking about you. Hell, I think I'm in love with you!

Carrick, giving up on work, swiveled around in his chair. He couldn't concentrate because Sadie's words were bouncing around his brain.

He had a hangover from hell because he'd tucked into a bottle of twelve-year-old whiskey from his father's famous, rare and expensive collection. He refused to feel guilty for throwing it down his throat because having his heart broken again should be accompanied by the soothing taste of rare, expensive whiskey.

But unfortunately, there was no difference in rotgut liquor and smooth whiskey the day after. They both made him feel like someone was taking a sledgehammer to his brain.

Crazy about you, think I'm in love with you, I trusted you, but you won't trust me.

Carrick placed his elbows on his knees and stared at the floor. Seeing a paper clip lying on the carpet, he picked it up and slowly unbent the wire.

He had refused to explain. He had asked her to make up her own mind about him. And he believed they'd turned a corner, that she saw him clearly. She'd trusted her intuition, trusted him to show her who he really was and she'd believed...

He hadn't.

What if what she was saying was true? What if she really wasn't going back to Paris? What if, instead of reacting, he'd sought to understand first and judge later?

First things first, he needed to know whether Sadie was leaving Boston, leaving him. He'd call Beth, get this straightened out...

Carrick sat up and reached for his phone, wondering if he still had his sister-in-law's number. He scrolled through his contacts. One call and he could have this straightened out...

But if he called Beth, he would be going through an intermediary, taking her word above Sadie's. If they had a chance to make this work, make *them* work, then he had to deal with Sadie. He had to work this out with her.

Calling Beth was the easy way out and he was still ducking the issue. The fundamental problem was trust. He either trusted Sadie...

Or he didn't.

He'd asked her to believe what he'd shown her; what if he did the same for her? What if he looked at her words and actions and made up his own mind, just as he'd asked her to do? Yeah, unfortunately, the boot didn't fit so easily when he shoved it onto his own foot.

Putting his phone back down on his desk, he

thought back over the past few weeks and forced himself to carefully examine all their interactions. Sadie had never, not once, lied to him. She worked long hours, prepared professional updates, kept their working life separate from their personal relationship. She'd told him about the baby; she hadn't hidden her pregnancy from him. She'd agreed they'd raise their child together; she'd told him she wanted her child to have as much of a full-time dad as he could manage to be.

She hadn't acted like she wanted to go back to Paris. In fact, the opposite was true. Her words, her innate affection and the way she looked at him told him that she was prepared, despite her lousy marriage, to take a chance on him.

And that she'd trusted him not to hurt her…

But he *had* hurt her and done it well. He'd seen it in her pale face, her tear-stained eyes, in her tight mouth. He'd wounded her and he wanted to kick his own ass. Despite the emotional abuse she'd experienced in her marriage, then the betrayal of her friends and family not believing her, she'd opened herself up to him, trusting him to have her back.

She'd been brave, but at the first little setback, he'd folded like a cheap pack of cards.

God, he couldn't be more ashamed of himself if he tried.

Hearing the tap on his door, he slowly turned around and saw Ronan in the doorway, his expression concerned.

"What's up?" he asked his brother, his tone curt.

"Marsha's canceled your meetings and is holding your calls. She's worried because the last time you cut yourself off so completely, Tanna had been in an accident."

That was the problem with an assistant who'd worked for him for so long. She knew him better than he knew himself. And his brother had the worst timing ever.

Carrick frowned at him. "And you didn't think that maybe I needed some time alone?"

Ronan came inside and closed the door. "But what you want and what you need are two totally separate things."

Right now Carrick needed to find Sadie, not sit through a lecture from his brother. They needed to work this out. And yes, that would include groveling on his part. He'd do what he'd have to do to make this right...

"I know what I need, Ronan."

"No, Carrick, you *think* you know. You think you want to be alone, to protect yourself from hurt, from having another woman leaving you. I hate to tell you this, but you can't control anyone's actions. People leave, people die and people mess up."

Carrick tipped his head to the side, thinking this was the most emotion he'd heard from Ronan in a long, long time. Wanting to see where this went, even if it meant delaying seeing Sadie, he gestured for him to keep speaking.

"You and Sadie ended it, didn't you? Or, to be more precise, you did."

Carrick shrugged, holding his brother's eye. He just nodded and noticed the frustration cross his brother's face. "She was your one, Carrick, the person meant for you. How could you not see that?"

Wow. Interesting that Ronan had noticed. "How do you know?"

"Because I know true love when I see it, Carrick! I lived it, I had it and I recognize it. She is your other half, the person you are supposed to be with."

"I thought the same with Tamlyn," Carrick said, knowing his feelings for Sadie couldn't be compared to what he felt for his ex. It was like comparing a dull beige with alizarin crimson, milk with cream, cut glass shards with diamonds.

But if his comment kept Ro talking...

"You don't only get one person to love and you love people differently, at different times of your life. You loved Tamlyn, but you're a different person now from the person who loved her. You don't only get one shot at marriage and love, Carrick."

Carrick held his brother's gaze, hiding his smile as Ronan walked into a trap of his own making. "I hear you, Ronan, I do."

Ronan released a sigh. "So you are going to sort out this mess with Sadie?"

"I am. But before I do, can I ask you one question?"

Ronan nodded, then shrugged. "Sure."

"Why is there one set of rules for me, but not for you? If I get to take another shot at a relationship, why can't you?"

Ronan's astonishment would, Carrick decided, always remain with him.

Since leaving Beth's a few hours before, and not being ready to return to her office at Murphy's—Sadie knew it would be weeks, maybe months, before she could face Carrick with equanimity again—she returned to her rented apartment and, sitting on the sofa with her laptop on the table in front of her, flipped through the scanned images of various documents she'd found at the Virginia Museum of Art and Culture.

If she didn't focus on work, she'd be consumed by thoughts of Carrick and she might, just might, be tempted to head back to Murphy's to beg him to believe her. She couldn't allow herself to do that.

Love, and trust, when not given freely, meant nothing at all.

So she'd buckle down. She'd do her job and after she submitted her final report she wouldn't have to see or talk to Carrick again. Not for a few months anyway. She had time before she had to introduce him to his child.

Maybe by then, her heart would've healed.

Ignoring that sharp pain in her chest, she forced herself to read the entries of a diary written by one of Winslow Homer's friends, concentrating on the spidery handwriting, looking for words that might be a reference to Homer, art or paintings. She was a third of the way through an entry when a passage caught her eye…

I watched Winslow work on the third of a series of paintings today detailing the lives of slave women on a plantation just south of here. He stood in the fields and watched the two children play, sketching rapidly. The detail took my breath away...the torn pocket on the girl child's pinafore, the faint scar above the boy's eyebrow...

Wait...

Sadie felt the thump of excitement, the taste of a breakthrough in her mouth. Scrabbling for a folder she'd left on the floor, she yanked it open, not caring when the papers inside fluttered to the ground. She didn't care about the documents; she needed the photographic reprint she'd made of the painting...

Sadie turned the photograph to the light coming from the lamp and—yes! Sadie punched the air with her fist.

The girl's pocket was torn; the boy did have a scar over his eyebrow...she had proof! It wasn't a solid provenance, but she was getting there and it was a lot more than she'd had before.

Sadie heard the knock on her door and, still holding the photograph, she walked into the small hallway to yank open the door.

The first thing she saw was a massive bunch of flowers and she instantly recognized the hand that held them. If Carrick thought she could be bribed by a bunch of flowers as an apology, he was in for a rude shock.

She pushed the flowers away to look up into his face, her Homer discovery instantly forgotten. He looked older than he had yesterday, drawn and wan. It was obvious that his night had been as horrible as hers but she wasn't angelic enough to feel bad about that.

He deserved to feel like an ass because he'd acted like one.

"What do you want?" she demanded, folding her arms and sending him a belligerent look.

He tried to push the flowers toward her, but she just narrowed her eyes. His hand, and the arrangement, dropped to his side. "Can I come in?"

"What's the point?"

Carrick looked like he was trying to hold on to his temper. "The point is that I have things to say and I'd prefer not to say them in the hallway."

Sadie just lifted her eyebrows and planted her feet. "I'd prefer you not to have acted like an ass, but we don't always get what we want, do we?"

Carrick looked up to the ceiling and sighed. "I should've realized this wouldn't be easy."

Sadie was tired, she was upset and she didn't have the energy to face the man who couldn't give her what she wanted. "Carrick, so far today I've spoken to Beth and to my parents. Neither conversation was easy. I'm upset and emotional and tired. Please just go."

"No."

Carrick then lifted his arms and the flowers flew past her head. Sadie turned and watched them land next to the coffee table, scattering leaves and petals on the beige carpet. "Did that make you feel better?" she asked the scowling Carrick.

"No, but this will." Carrick gripped her hips, pulled her into him and covered her lips with his.

Sadie didn't even try to resist. Her anger dissipated as his tongue twirled around hers, as he placed his hand behind her head to hold her still. Kissing Carrick was all she wanted to do for the rest of her life, but she couldn't do it on and off, on a friends-with-benefits basis. She needed his love, his trust, his commitment. She needed what he didn't have to give.

Sadie pushed her hands against his chest and Carrick immediately released her. Walking back into her apartment, Sadie bit down on her bottom lip and stared at him, feeling like her heart was being ripped in two. "I can't do this, Carrick."

"Why not?"

"Because I need love, I need your trust, I need... everything."

Carrick nodded. "Okay."

He was too quick to agree, too fast off the line. "That wasn't how you felt last night."

Carrick nodded, and Sadie realized that his eyes were a shade of green she'd never seen before. It was like there was a gold flame burning behind his irises, allowing them to glow. "As you pointed out, last night I was an ass. Today I hope I am a little less of an ass."

"Stop talking in riddles and say what you came to say," Sadie snapped.

Carrick nodded, sat down on the edge of the closest chair and crossed one ankle over his knee. He sent her a steady look, a look that was full of—dare she believe it?—love.

"When I told Tamlyn I wanted a divorce, she went a little nuts. What I thought would be an amicable split turned into a living nightmare. She didn't want to be married to me, but she sure as hell didn't want me leaving her, either. And she wanted to punish me. She went after my house, the art, the company. It was all stipulated in the prenup so she couldn't touch any of it. Stories started appearing in the press and they always occurred within a few days of a meeting with our lawyers…and always when she didn't get her way."

Carrick was explaining his past; he was opening up. Sadie dropped to the nearest chair, scared to say anything in case he stopped talking.

"The more she lost, the more she wanted to hurt me. I had threatening calls, threatening text messages. Believe it or not, she egged my house. She eventually calmed down when I threatened her with a restraining order. But the rumors kept on coming. My siblings wanted me to take her on about what she was saying, but I refused to let them. People would either believe her or me and I sure as hell wasn't going to beg them to believe me.

"I didn't care what anyone thought until you came along," Carrick added, his voice low and his words saturated with emotion. "I expected you to trust me without explanation, but I couldn't do the same for you. So with your permission, I'm going to try that conversation from yesterday again…"

Sadie tipped her head, keeping her fingers tightly knotted.

"Sadie, I heard you might be going back to Paris. Is that true?"

Sadie shook her head. "No. It's a long story why Beth thought it important to renew my lease instead of canceling it as I asked her to do, but no, I'm staying in Boston. One of my to-do items is finding an apartment or home in Boston, preferably a two-bedroom place so I can have a nursery."

The tension seeped out of Carrick as he played with the laces on his shoe. "I know of a pretty big house where you could have your choice of bedrooms for a nursery."

Sadie pretended to misunderstand him. "Really, where?"

He sent her a you're-messing-with-me look. "In Beacon Hill. Unfortunately, the offer comes with a couple of provisos. You'd have to share my bed, and I'd expect to put my ring on your finger at some point."

Sadie leaned forward, her arms on her thighs. It was all she wanted, but it wasn't enough. "Are you offering to marry me because I need a place to stay or because I'm having your child?"

"I want to marry you because I can't imagine not marrying you, not living with you, not having you as the center of my life. I want you to live with me because I can't imagine my life without you in it. I'm crazy mad in love with you, Dr. Slade."

Sadie wanted to believe him; she really did. She wanted to fall into the hope blooming in her chest, to trust what he was telling her was the truth. But she was scared, so scared of being disappointed by him again.

"You and I, we're a team, Sades. I messed up yesterday big-time, but I am asking you one more time to trust in me, to trust in us. When you fall down, I'll pick you up. When somebody comes for you, I want to be the one who stands between you and the world. When you have a bad day, I want to be the one to give you a good night. I'll be there, Sadie, every step of the way. I promise to love you through everything life throws at us."

Sadie felt that hard layer of ice surrounding her heart crack and fall away, felt her stomach slip out of its tangled knot. Then Carrick held out his hand, and Sadie placed hers in his, emotion burning as she finally, finally realized she was home. Wherever Carrick was. She'd never be alone again.

She was, as he said, part of a team.

Carrick's hand tightened around hers and he gave her a yank, pulling her into his arms. Scooping her up to sit on his lap, her legs straddling his thighs, he held her face and stared deeply into her eyes. "I love you, sweetheart. I'm so sorry I disappointed you. Please give me, give *us*, another chance."

Sadie traced his eyebrow with one finger. "I love you, too."

"That's good to hear, but that's still not a yes on my let's-give-us-another-chance question," Carrick said, his voice gentle. "I need to know, Sades."

"Yes, Carrick. To everything."

Carrick's shoulders slumped and Sadie felt the last

of his tension leave his body. Then he picked up her hand and tugged. Sadie looked down and saw she was still holding the printout of the painting and she remembered her fantastic news. "Carrick, I found something! It's amazing news... Homer definitely painted this—"

Carrick placed his hand over her mouth, his eyes filled with joy. "Sweetheart, I realize I am always going to have to compete with art for your attention, but right now, can I not?" His hands dropped to the edges of her sweater and he slowly, deliberately pulled it up her body. "You, Sadie Slade, are my greatest treasure, my best canvas, my favorite piece of art. And I intend to spend the next sixty years reminding you of that every damn day."

Sadie allowed the photograph to drift to the floor. He was right; this was their time. Her news could wait.

The celebration of their love could not.

Epilogue

Sadie, in the boardroom of Murphy International, couldn't take the huge smile off her face. She was in love, carrying her man's child, she'd had amazing sex this morning—and last night—and she'd never been happier in her life.

And now she got to tell Keely and Joa that not only did she think their painting was by Homer—the results of the paint analysis informed her that the paints used on the canvas were consistent with paints used in the mid-nineteenth century and also with Homer's preferences—but that there were another two paintings in the series.

Where were they? She couldn't wait to start tracking them down…she was damn good at her job.

As she'd proved when she finally tracked down the

artist of the massive painting in Carrick's—no, their bedroom. Between researching the Homer paintings, she'd flipped through countless databases of unattributed works and finally found a similar canvas in a private collection in Dubai, a collection she'd had the privilege of viewing, via Hassan's father, years ago.

The painting was by Joshua Reynolds, who was better known for portraits than for landscapes.

Yeah, let's be honest, she rocked at tracking down provenance and attributions.

She was nearly as good at that as she was at loving Carrick Murphy...

Sadie stood behind Carrick, needing to feel his heat, his presence, their connection. Looking down at him, she smiled. She was so lucky to have him in her life; their child was blessed to have him as their father...

Carrick looked up as his hand covered the hand on his shoulder. "Are you okay, sweetheart?"

Sadie nodded, suddenly emotional. "Very okay."

"You're not going to faint again, are you?"

She grinned since he often teased her about falling at his feet. "Not right now."

Carrick lifted his arm to encircle her waist. "Not very professional, Mr. Murphy," Sadie murmured.

"I can't tell you how little I care," Carrick replied.

"Jeez, not only do I have to watch Levi and Tanna's public displays of affection, I now have to watch you two, as well?" Ronan complained as he walked into the room. "Unhand your fiancée, brother, we have work to do."

Sadie looked down at her engagement ring—sapphires and diamonds—and grinned. She was Carrick's fiancée and would, when they finally decided on whether to get married before or after their baby's birth, be his wife. She couldn't wait.

But Ronan was right; they had work to do, so she stepped away from Carrick and smiled at Keely and Joa. "I have good news and better news. The good news is that I'm convinced your painting is a Homer."

Joa's eyes immediately darted to Ronan, and they exchanged a look full of heat and a healthy dose of confusion. Sadie looked at Carrick and raised her eyebrows. He winked at her, telling her that he also noticed the sparks flying between his brother and his nanny.

Keely clapped her hands in glee. "Take that, Wilfred." She looked at Carrick. "Wilfred was convinced it was a fake. I can't wait to tell him he was *wrong, wrong, wrong.*"

Sadie had heard that the estate was wound up, so why were Keely and her lawyer still talking? Especially since they seemed to rub each other the wrong way. And why did she call him Wilfred when everyone else called him Dare?

Anyway, back to business.

"The better news is that I think it's one of a series. There are two more paintings out there. The one you own might be copies of the originals."

Joa leaned forward. "If we own one original, where are the other two?"

Sadie lifted her hands. "Good question. Somebody needs to track them down."

Joa glanced at Keely before a beautiful smile crossed her face and brightened her eyes. "Can we hire you to do that?"

Sadie grinned, and mentally punched the air. She'd wanted to suggest that the Mounton-Matthews heirs do exactly that, but she hadn't wanted to sound too pushy. Of course, if they hadn't asked, she would've offered.

"Of course I will. I'm not walking away now." Sadie looked across the table to Carrick, who was watching her with a lazy, sexy, possessive look on his face. She tipped her head to one side and gently rested her hand on her slightly rounded stomach. "I'm not ever walking away again."

Carrick smiled at her. "Good to know. Not that I'd let you but still…good to know. Now come here and kiss me."

Ronan released a long, heartfelt groan. "Oh, for the love of God, enough already!"

Never, Sadie thought, as she walked over to Carrick. She'd never get enough of him and his love and the life they were in the process of creating.

And, judging by the way Carrick looked at her, neither would he.

* * * * *